THE WORST NOELLE

ANNA FOXKIRK

THE WORST NOELLE
by Anna Foxkirk

Copyright©AnnaFoxkirk2023

All rights reserved. No part of this book may be reproduced or used in any manner without written permission of the copyright owner except for the use of quotations in a book review.

This is a work of fiction. Names, characters, places and incidents are either the product of the author's imagination or are used fictitiously. Any resemblance to actual persons, living or dead, events or locales is entirely coincidental.

First published in 2021.
ISBN:

Published by Flock Press.

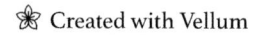

❦ Created with Vellum

The Worst Noelle is dedicated to my beloved family who make every Christmas the best!

1

The novelty of slumming it wears off after about ten minutes of traveling economy. There's no elbow space. There's no leg space. Once I helped the little old lady sitting in front of me to put her bag in the overhead locker, there's not even Balenciaga bag space. I am forced to squish my precious bag under my seat.

I get the air stewardess's attention. "Um, excuse me, I know you're busy, but is there another seat available that I could move to which has a little more...um...space, please?"

Her expression pinches. "Is there a problem?" She looks pointedly at the men sitting either side of me.

"Oh no! It's not that. It's just that I'm a little cramped. I wondered if there might be a seat with some more room, perhaps one that actually reclined—"

"These seats have limited reclining because they're in front of the lavatories," she explains with a sour expression on her face. "There was the option to select your seat when you booked your flight, madam." She annunciates every word as if I am an idiot.

I feel like I've just had my knuckles rapped. I smile at her, though I would like to strangle her with her natty nylon neck scarf. "No, really. You call this *limited*?"

Her mouth pouts, and I bite my lip.

Crap. Did I sound like my mother just then? Rude and obnoxious and entitled? "I apologize, I'm just not used to this." Fuck. That sounds even worse. This is the worst!

By the time I'd gotten round to booking my flights there hadn't exactly been many seat options left, and besides, after drowning my woes in a bottle of Beaujolais, I'd been in no fit state to make carefully considered decisions. After retrieving the wedding invitation from the trash, I'd impulsively bought my tickets and only then rung Lara in New Zealand to let her know the good news. "Hey, Lara! It's me!"

"Noelle?" she'd groaned. "What the...what time is it?"

I took another gulp of my wine, valiantly fighting off the first pincer grip of hangover. "Sorry, did I wake you babe?"

"Mmm. Don't worry. How are you? Is something wrong?"

Don't even get me started. Everything is wrong, the life I have fought so damn hard to build unraveling faster than toilet paper. "No, I have great news to share, and it couldn't wait. I had to let you know, I've changed my mind. There's no way I'm going to miss your wedding. I just booked my flight to New Zealand!"

There's a howling silence. For a moment I think I've lost the connection. "Lara? Lara? Are you still there?"

"Sorry. Did I hear that right? You're coming to New Zealand after all?"

"Yes! That's what I just said. Why? Would you rather I wasn't?"

"No! Of course, not, silly. I'm just a little surprised, is all." I hear shuffling and someone grumbling in the background. Probably her fiancé. I can't believe I haven't even met the guy. I can't believe she's getting married before me.

"I thought you said it was too far to come and you were crazy busy at work right now." When am I ever not crazy busy at work? "And, you had to spend Christmas with your family, like always."

Of all the lame excuses. Of course, I could be flying home to the Hamptons right now, wallowing in Foley festive luxury — but, that always comes with a generous chaser of family bickering. Instead, because of my impulsive, and what my dad calls my bone-headed attitude, here I am being spat through the air like a cat's hairball on route to my best friend's wedding.

A best friend I haven't seen for over five years...and rarely speak to these days.

But our pervious conversation had been over a month ago and a lot can happen in a month. "I was always planning on coming," I say. "I just had to figure out the details."

"I wasn't expecting it, but that's awesome news! I can't wait to see you, Noelle!"

I hear more mumbling in the background, then Lara whispering, telling someone to go back to sleep.

It was only the next day, in the sour light of morning with a vicious hangover for company, as I tried to unpick the previous night's drinking spree and decidedly flighty decisions, that I wondered if I hadn't screwed up. Again. Had Lara sounded a mite unenthusiastic about my impending visit and us rekindling our bestie status? Maybe I should've called her first to check she still wanted me to come. Maybe she would've preferred a generous wedding gift, rather than my heroic gesture—something decadent from her wedding gift list such as the electric sheepshearing handpiece...

Or, maybe not.

Let's be honest, I haven't seen Lara in five years and, if a lot can happen in a month, imagine how much can change in half a decade. It's somewhat concerning, but too late to rectify.

I am now on a flight bound for New Zealand, the land of the long white cloud. That doesn't sound to me like the most promising sort of holiday or very good marketing. Who needs any more clouds in their life, especially not super long ones? If this is not true loyalty and dedication to our enduring friendship, I don't know what is.

"Any chance of a drink any time soon?" I plead with the air stewardess. I know I shouldn't have another drink, but flying always makes me nervous as hell. "After our delay, perhaps we should be entitled to a little compensation." I smile cheekily. "A glass of champagne would not go amiss..."

The air stewardess pouts. "I'm sorry, ma'am, but there will be no drinks served until after the fasten-your-seatbelt signs have been switched off. You do realize that drinks are not free in this section of the plane?"

Do I look like I can't pay?

"Of course, I realize." As if I need reminding. We will probably have to pay for toilet paper just to wipe our asses. Do I *seriously* look like I can't pay? "I just thought, um, it would be a nice gesture..."

Clearly, the air stewardess disagrees as she's already sashaying off along the aisle.

"Oh shoot!" It's not exactly an auspicious start to my escape abroad. "Someone put me out of my misery."

"Perhaps not the smartest thing to say on a plane," says the man sitting next to me. "Shoot."

I turn to give him a frosty glare, but his eyes are fixed on his ebook.

"I was joking, *obviously*," I say.

Neither of my traveling companions react. I am squished between a rock and a hard place ... actually, more like a rock and a mushroom. Man Mountain in the window seat, ever since giving me a rigorous double take — because clearly women wearing Armani suits are seldom seen in cattle class — is now studiously ignoring me. Man Mushroom on my left whose arm and elbow are overlapping my armrest has already fallen asleep, mouth gaping wide enough to stow a carry-on suitcase.

Gawwwd. You know how they call these flights *long haul* ... the best way to endure such prolonged torture is steeped in alcohol. But *why* hadn't I paid for Business or First Class? Oh yes. Because there hadn't been a seat available, not for love nor money. Money isn't an issue. Being stuck here for twelve hours without anyone to take my mind off the fact we are hurtling forty plus thousand feet or thereabouts above the ground is. What warped part of my brain had informed me this would be a wonderful idea? A cocktail-induced coma could have made better choices than me.

It's enough to make me break out in hives.

I scratch my neck.

"Good book?" I lean toward the Rock in the window seat.

"Mmmhmm." Above his spectacles, his brow knits. I have to be honest, he has it worse than either Mushroom Man or me. He must be well over six foot and Rock's denim-clad knees are mashed hard up against the seat in front. If I wasn't locked in a silent battle for elbow space, I might (almost) feel sorry for him, but he also lost my vote of sympathy the moment he stole the armrest.

I guess chivalrous behavior doesn't extend beyond Business Class.

Traveling economy is the sort of remedial torture Lara would approve of. From what I can gather, she's become terrifyingly virtuous, practically a saint, having given everything up to be with the man she loves. Shaun. Shaun, ugh! The name conjures up sheep shearing and gum boots. The truth is Lara getting married seemed to pour oil onto the fire of my already messed up, usually highly business-focused, brain. I panic-bought those plane tickets, and as we all know, panic-shopping is never a good idea. Nothing like the benefit of hindsight…but unless there's an eject button it's a little too late to extract myself.

A shudder travels through me. "You'd think after the waiting and all, they'd have provided us with a beverage." I pull out the inflight magazine and with my elbows tucked into my sides like chicken wings, I flick through the pages pretending to be enthralled —Who even buys this crap? It's so overpriced. Meanwhile, the harrowing realization I'm stuck on this plane getting farther and farther away from civilization and closer and closer to what is most likely to be … the worst wedding, the worst Christmas, the worst mistake ever is beginning to make me feel nauseous.

I reach for the paper vomit bag. "Don't worry. I'll be fine," I say to no-one in particular.

Don't get me wrong. I still love Lara despite our losing touch. We have history together. At school we'd been like magnets, practically attached at the hip, living in one another's pockets … but also, if I'm being totally honest, we also sometimes repelled one another. We grew up in the Pacific Palisades, went to the same private school, liked the same music, but our tastes in pretty much everything could not have been more diametrically opposed. One of the bonuses of that was we never clashed over potential boyfriends or any aspirations for the future. Well, Lara didn't really have aspirations. I was the one with the big dreams.

Once we'd left the closeted existence of high school, Lara and I had gone our separate ways: I'd thrown myself into university and a career, and Lara threw herself into the void — she wanted to see the world. It makes me cringe thinking about some of the whacky and wild stuff she's done over the years from being blessed on one of the floating villages of Lake Titicaca to learning to pole dance in Beijing. I kid you not. That is where she'd met Shaun. Lara used to send me postcards...until one day I received one saying she had found 'the one and only', her 'true love' and decided to stay in New Zealand.

That had come as something of a shock. For two years we didn't write or speak at all. Then the wedding invitation had arrived along with a photo of her and Shaun and a letter asking me to be her maid-of-honor. It had about as much appeal as swallowing the worm in the tequila.

Talking of which, where the heck is my drink? I shove the magazine and barf bag back where they should be. Only eleven hours and fifty five minutes more to endure ...

On my left, Man Mushroom lets rip with a beer-bellied snore and one of his shirt buttons pops off almost taking my eye out.

"Are you kidding?!" I mutter.

Leg room is not an issue for Mushroom Man. He's shorter than I am. In the airport lounge, at opposite ends of the bar, we'd pretty much matched one another round for round of drinks. We'd even got talking about his ex-wife, her new partner, and his two kids on their expensive ski trip to Canada. For a while, I felt sorry for him spending Christmas alone ... until I was seated next to him. The fact he's now infringing on my already *limited* space, especially if he's going to snore the entire way to Christchurch, is fast becoming a significant issue. Most of all, I resent the fact that the alcohol we'd both consumed in the bar isn't having quite the same anesthetic effects on me as it evidently is on him. And his brand of snoring is like being run through with a hacksaw.

I rifle through the pocket of the seat in front of me again. "Did you get any earphones? I don't have any earphones. Did I miss out on that handout?"

Man Mountain's eyes flicker in my direction. He huffs, but I swear he splays his knees wider.

"Excuse me. Could you just...?" I corkscrew toward him with my knees, but when he finally decides to pay me any attention, the look he gives me would crack ice. Seriously? His knee doesn't budge and his expression has as much sympathy as a ... rock face.

"Do *you* mind?" he asks, deadpan.

"Yeah, I do mind, actually!" More than he could possibly imagine. It's a tough call not to feel sorry for myself, stuck between the Hacksaw and the Rock, twisted like a goddamn contortionist trying to fit myself into a shoebox with nothing better to do for the next goddamn-how-many hours than mull over the sinkhole of my life. Talk about adding torment to torture. "I know this isn't easy for you, being tall and all, but strictly speaking your knee is encroaching on my space. See here. This is where your space ends." I draw a line in the air from the edge of my seat to his splayed knee. I give his kneecap a poke with my fingernail.

Rock sighs, exasperation tattooed all over his face. "What do you expect me to do about it?"

"Go and sit elsewhere?" I suggest.

His eyebrows rise. I suppose that was a little rude, but his inertia does little to ease the hive of frustration building beneath my skin. So what? He's not impressed with my attitude, but he's not exactly Mr Sympathetic, and, unfortunately for him, he's making my unbearable situation worse.

As I wriggle, his lips compress into a thin line. His knees do not budge even one millimeter. I increase the pressure of my knee against his like it's some sort of competition.

I press the Call button for the air hostess again. And again. And again.

"Careful, you might break a fingernail," says the Rock.

Wow.

Is he trying to intimidate me? "I might break more than that," I snap temporarily forgetting the knee competition. He gains a centimeter.

Bastard.

His eyes are focused on whatever he's reading, but his lips twitch.

Seriously? Bastard!

"I don't think my call button works. Could I try yours?" Without waiting for an answer, I reach over and press his call button.

"You sure you wouldn't like to put your feet up while you're at it. Perhaps you'd like a foot massage." He doesn't smile.

"Ha.Ha. From you? I'd rather put my foot in an animal trap."

"No-one's going to come. As the lady said, you have to wait until the fasten-your-seatbelt lights have been extinguished."

The plane gives a shudder.

"Woah! What the hell was that?"

The Rock is unperturbed and ignores me.

"If I don't get a drink soon, I'm going to be doing some extinguishing of my own. This is the worst flight ever. The worst everything!"

"Ladies and gentlemen, please remain seated with your seatbelts fastened. We're anticipating flying into some turbulence," says the pilot over the speakers.

"Oh great. That's not good. How many more hours of this torture do they expect us to endure? No, don't tell me, I don't want to know." I scrabble around beneath the seat muttering to myself. "Should've flown Business Class. This is what comes of making impulsive decisions. Never again!"

Pushing my hair out of my face, I brandish a bottle of champagne. "Ha! Never fear. This calls for duty free." Even though I'd bought the bottle to give to Lara, she'll understand an emergency of this nature. "Would you be so kind as to pop the cork? Oh, darn, we don't have glasses. What the hell, I'm traveling economy, it wouldn't be inappropriate to drink straight of the bottle. Would it?"

Rock looks at me as if I have grown two heads. He makes no move to take the bottle from my hand.

"I'm not contaminated, if that's what you're worried about. Anyway, if I were, it's too late for you we couldn't get much closer." I smile. Warmly. " Any chance of a hand opening this? I'll share."

"No thank you," he says, then distinctly mutters something about a high maintenance *princess*...

My mouth drops open. Did my ears just deceive me? "I presume you're not reading a fairytale in that book. Did you just call me a Princess? You...you...uhhh! How rude!" I glare at him, then stuff my bottle back in my duty free bag.

He's got his eyes glued to his book, but a goddamn irritating smile dances about his lips.

From his accent, I've gathered he's clearly a New Zealander ... or at any rate most definitely Neanderthal. To be honest, I can never quite distinguish between the Australian and New Zealand accent. Wherever he's from, he's damn offensive, and in my family we've been well-trained in the area of being offensive, believe you me. "What gives you the right to call someone you don't even know a princess?"

Our eyes clash again. I have to admit, his are actually somewhat arresting. Pale grey, ringed with black. "Put it this way, from the way you've been fidgeting for the last hour and that bottle of Cristal, not to mention all the bellyaching you've been doing, I don't get the impression you're used to roughing it, darl. Not at all. A prime example of the pea and the *princess*." His smile doesn't reach his eyes.

I suck in a breath. I'm actually weirdly kind of flattered which confuses me, but I know how to look affronted. I arch an eyebrow. "You know what, an apology would be nice."

"I agree," he says.

"I'm s-sorry?" I splutter.

"Apology accepted. Now if you don't mind"— He lifts his book— "this is interesting." And he resumes reading.

"That was *not* an apology from me. *You* are the one who should be apologizing."

I am ignored.

His open disregard for me is disconcerting. It's another alarming sign that I'm losing my grip on reality.

Up until three months ago, I felt invincible — on top of the world, on top of my job, on top of my man — Cole. Now my life is a dungheap and the crap is piled so high on top of me I can barely breathe. I am literally suffocating. Like it's a truly good-for-nothing day when someone as ordinary as the Rock is immune to my feminine charms. It doesn't take a mind-reader to see he a) doesn't find me remotely attractive b) disapproves of my *everything* c) is not a gentleman d) is not the slightest bit interested in my welfare, and e) wishes he'd chosen to sit anywhere else other than next to the highly-strung wreckage taking up space in 49 B.

"I am not a princess!" I whine. Far from it. I have had to make sacrifices to get to the top. I'm beginning to worry if those sacrifices were worth it. I groan as I rifle through the contents of my handbag. The only remedy I come up with is some Rose Hibiscus Face Mist. "Well, this flight is going to be a joy, isn't it?" I say spritzing liberally. "Are all New Zealanders like you?"

"Like what?"

I show him my perfect teeth. They are worth every cent. "Like totally lacking in manners or sensitivity."

The bastard smiles back. He also has perfect teeth. "Shit, yeah."

"Look, clearly this is not an ideal situation...but if we're going to be stuck cheek to jowl for the next twelve hours, we could at least try to be civil to one another, don't you think?" I say, magicking some diplomatic charm from somewhere.

"Does that involve being spritzed?"

"You're hilarious." I purse my lips and put my spritzer away. "I'm Noelle. Noelle Foley." I offer my hand. "And you are ...?"

"Sam Devine."

I laugh. Perhaps a little too hard. "*Divine*. That's hilarious! I mean, that's your surname? How unusual. For real that's your surname?"

"D.*E*.V.I.N.E," he spells out, stressing the e.

"So, Mr *De*-vine. What do you do when you're not being a—"

The plane suddenly drops two feet.

"—*jeeeeerk!*" My stomach hits my throat. We lurch upwards again and another yelp escapes me. I brace myself against the seat in front. The growl of the engines increases to a deafening roar.

"Perhaps the issues they were having before we took off didn't entirely get fixed," he says.

"Oh, gee, thanks for that little newsflash. Great to know. How reassuring—"

"Please remain seated and ensure your seatbelts are fastened," intones the pilot.

"Like we're going anywhere!" I squeak.

The plane drops again—it could be five feet, it could be fifty.

"Arrrrggg!" I yelp and grab hold of the armrests only to realize my nails are digging into flesh and bone. I should remove my hands, I know I should, but right now the plane is shaking us around like it's trying to make cocktails.

"Oh, no, this is not good....Oh fucking hell!" I whimper.

We're buffeted and tossed. The engine whine rises to a crescendo.

I squeeze my eyes closed. "Distract me. Talk to me. Say something. De-*vine!*" The last syllable is a shriek as we plummet once more.

"Do you have a phobia of flying by any chance?" Sam's voice is ridiculously calm.

"No! Just a phobia of dying!"

"There is a one in three point three billion chance of dying in a commercial airplane crash and over ninety-eight per cent of plane crashes don't result in fatality," says Sam.

"Terrific! How's that meant to make me feel any better? What are you, an actuary? Oh, for the love of—!"

"What's happening?" Even Man Mushroom has risen from the dead.

"Just some turbulence. We'll be fine," says Sam, casual as you like.

"You don't know that! This isn't just ordinary turbulence! I'm not fine!" My stomach careens as we drop downward again. "I can't stand this. I can't. Why did I think going to New Zealand for my best friend's wedding was a great idea? I must've been out of my mind. I am so sorry. Whatever I did to deserve this, I'm so, so sorry. If you're listening God..."

"Take a few deep breaths. I think we're through the worst of it," says Sam.

I gulp, but can't seem to get enough air in my lungs.

"Seriously. It's alright. It's easing up."

I open one eye. He could be right. The jumping around seems to have petered out and the engines have settled into a steady rhythm again.

"You can let go of me now," says Sam.

I look at his forearm — "Oh. God. Sorry!" — and unhook my nails. I've dug white crescents into his skin.

"Could be worse," he says, rubbing his forearm.

"Yeah, we could've died. You two could be the last two people I ever talk to. That was scary as hell. I need a drink more than ever. Right now. Seatbelt signs on or not." I press the call button again. "How come you're so damn calm?"

He pushes his reading glasses up his nose. "Well, I have to deal with some fairly challenging situations in my line of work."

"You're not an actuary?" I say.

He goes back to reading his book.

"So, go on. Tell me. What do you do for a living?"

"Nothing that would interest you." He doesn't look up.

"You never know. I might be fascinated. Why the reticence? You're not one of those covert air marshals, are you? Oh shit. Please tell me you're not!"

He snorts. "Not quite. I'm a stunt coordinator."

I do a double take. "Bullshit! You're winding me up. Get out of here!"

"That's not really an option."

"A stuntman? You are not!"

He shrugs and smiles ruefully. "Afraid so."

As I sit up in my seat and pay a bit more attention to his penetrating gray eyes, cashmere grey jumper and jean-clad thighs, I register that everything about him is understated. He does kind of look as if he might be in great physical shape for that line of work. Possibly.

"Hmm! But you don't actually do the stunts yourself? You coordinate them."

He opens his book again. "I wouldn't ask anyone to do something I wasn't prepared to do myself. I test all the stunts out first. Often I end up doing them myself."

"Wow. I've never met a…stuntman. You don't look…I mean, I'm… actually…surprised." I shake my head. Seriously? As well as being somewhat understated, he's got this nerdy vibe going on, what with the reading glasses and all. "So, while the rest of us were crapping our pants, just now, you were like, this is just another day's work at the office…"

The upper lip twitches. "Not exactly. I don't like the unexpected any more than the next person."

I fold my arms and give him a slight nudge. "Go on. Tell me more. I'm intrigued."

"It's really not that interesting. This is." He indicates the book he's reading.

"Please. It's interesting to *me*, and it kind of looks like the air stewardess could be some time, and I really need something to distract me. What stunt are you working on now? Are you making a movie in New Zealand?"

He sighs and closes his book.

I sense he's holding back as he tells me minor details about the latest film he's involved in in the States, doubling for Tom Dorsey. I've no idea who he's talking about, until he mentions a big franchise blockbuster movie.

"Oh, that Tom Dorsey!"

The air stewardess finally brings around the drinks trolley and I'm so engrossed by his story, I nearly miss her. For the next hour, while Mushroom resumes his hacksaw snoring, Sam and I chat. I tell him stuff about me I wouldn't normally dream of telling a stranger, but it's good to get everything off my chest, and it's not like I'll ever see him again.

Maybe I also feel a little bit smug that I'm conversing with this seemingly ordinary, somewhat extraordinary, guy, and I've managed to draw him out of his shell, and we've practically bonded. Having survived the turbulence, I like to think of Sam Devine and me like comrades-in arms. I open up the camera on my phone and surreptitiously take a couple of selfies with Sam in the background and me holding a glass of bubbling champagne in the foreground. Then I ruin it by knocking my drink flying.

Sam catches the glass mid-air — Of course, he does. Lightning-speed reflexes — saving it from spilling all over the pair of us.

"Oops! Wow, almost superhuman!" Maybe I want to impress him. Maybe I've had one too many drinks. Maybe I feel it's time I lived life on the edge. "Sorry. I'm not normally so clumsy." Truth be told, I have topped up my alcohol levels and have a nice buzz going on again, thank you very much. "But it's been a hell of a month. It's like all these factors beyond my control are in cahoots, determined to make me give up my career and marry a Forbes Four Hundred like my parents would like, but I'm not that kind of girl, you know? Nor, before you say anything, am I the princess you think I am, by the way."

"Is that right?" From the teasing glint in his eyes, he clearly doesn't believe me.

"No. I'm fiercely independent. A career woman. The last thing I want is to be looked after or to settle down…especially somewhere like New Zealand!" I roll my eyes and then remember who I'm talking to. "Sorry, no offense, Kiwi, but Lara, my best friend, is marrying a farmer called Shaun and settling down in New Zealand, like forever." I can't help but grimace. "Not that I've anything against *him* per se. I've never even met the guy, or been to New Zealand for that matter, but personally, I can't imagine anything worse. It's like miles from anywhere … from anywhere in America…that is…" I trail off because of the way he's turned around in his seat and is studding me with narrowed his eyes is unnerving. "I've nothing against New Zealanders in general," I say.

"Just me and what was this dude's name again?" he asks.

"Shaun," I say, flicking through the photos on my phone.

"It seems a long way to come for a wedding you don't want to go to and to see a friend you barely speak to," he says. "You could have saved yourself the time, effort and dollars."

"Oh, I'm not worried about the money, and I couldn't say no to Lara. She's my best friend. Once upon a time we were inseparable and she's always been there for me, so now I need to return the favor. I'm loyal like that."

"Plus, absence makes the heart grow fonder. Right?"

"Exactly!"

"I was talking about your ex-boyfriend situation."

I frown and put my phone down.

"Isn't that what you said? Your ex, Cole, could show you a little more appreciation. He's behaves like you're just at his beck and call. He makes inappropriate demands—"

"Yes, alright!" Maybe I shouldn't have unburdened myself to Sam quite so freely. "But it's true. He doesn't appreciate me and everything I do for him."

"Imagine! How on earth could that even be possible?" His eyes widen, mocking me.

"Quit teasing. I'm telling you, what we had could've been great, but he took advantage. If you have something good you should nurture it and instead he ... he used me. Me! But I still miss... I still miss..." My voice quavers and I stop myself. The way Sam is looking at me suggests I'm sharing a little too much. I must stop talking about my work and relationship problems because he's going to think I'm a loser, plus with tears pricking and my throat swelling, I can hardly swallow my drink. "Let's hope this wedding's not a total train wreck. Unlike me, Lara always had lousy taste in men."

"Oh, you have impeccable taste where men are concerned?" He smirks.

"Well, not as shocking as Lara's. Her taste in guys always sucked. I hate to think what this guy she's marrying is going to be like. They met at some seedy pole-dancing club in China, so forgive me for sounding precocious, but I do *not* have high hopes."

Sam says nothing. He has closed his eyes. "Mmm. Sorry, sounds like a match made in heaven to me."

"Or hell." I'm irritated by his lack of sympathy. "Why are you so... so...goddamn..." I glare at him.

One of his eyes pops open. "So goddamn...?"

Disinterested in me! Disengaged with this conversation! Discombobulating! But I can hardly say that. I purse my lips. "Unemotional."

Both eyes open. "You want me to act emotional about your friend's fiancé?"

"No, it's not that. I'm just a little stressed about this whole situation and you're not really helping."

Frown lines appear between his brows. "Forgive me, I didn't realize this flight was your personal therapy session. And all things considered, I'm hardly the person you should spill your guts to. You don't know me, remember. Probably a good thing too, Princess." He closes his eyes again.

Boy, he may be handsome but he's irritating. "It must be hard being so perfect."

"Not so *hard* as you'd like to imagine," he mumbles.

In the silence that follows, much as I try to blot him out, my imagination runs riot while I fantasize about Sam being *hard*. I can't help checking out his crotch. Oh. Wow. As far as endowments go, he looks very well — what the hell am I doing?! I fix my eyes on the back of the seat in front and try to steer my thoughts toward Cole.

My dear ex accused *me* of being vanilla, but I'm not. I'm just particular. And busy. For an indulgent moment, I imagine Sam and I recklessly abseiling together from a burning building, Cole going up in smoke inside. And me in a jungle slung over Sam's shoulder fireman-style, Cole floundering around in his suit being eaten by crocodiles. And then Sam and I settling down, my head in the nook of his shoulder, reading a book together...

Yeah, my brain is most definitely fried.

But for some reason Sam has piqued my interest; they say still waters run deep. I bet beneath Sam's rough exterior there are some strong undercurrents. He's a *stuntman* for crying out loud. Like maybe he's even in the Mile High Club. He wouldn't give a shit about what anyone thought of him, and part of me wishes I could be more like that. More how Cole wants me to be — less vanilla, unfettered by fear (or *fettered* depending on the circumstances) and more open to trying new experiences.

Like the mile-high club.

I glance at Sam. I bet he's been there and done that.

Wild and reckless. Hmmm.

I nudge Sam with my elbow. "Before I let you go to sleep, can I ask you one last thing?"

"Hrrummph." His head rolls on the headrest to face me. His eyes are the same soft cashmere grey as his jumper. It may be my champagne-goggles now blurring his features or my frazzled brain misfiring, but I have the strongest urge to ruffle his dark brown hair just to see exactly how soft it is and how impervious he is to my touch. Not that I'd do anything like that to a complete stranger for real. I'm just curious.

"You're a man who lives life on the edge, aren't you?" I ask quietly.

A dimple lines his left cheek. "Is that your question?"

"No. Don't take what I'm about to say the wrong way."

"Oh-kaaaaay. Take what the wrong way?"

"What I'm about to ask you. But if I don't ask, I'll never know, right? That is ..."

The slight flicker of his mouth and his searching gaze almost dissuade me from asking anything at all. "I was wondering, if you'd ever ... Um, talking of stunts... Have you ever ...?" Oh God. His eyes are boring into me. Maybe this isn't such a good idea.

"Spit it out, Princess."

The heat rises to my cheeks. Maybe I am vanilla with a capital V after all. If I can't even ask a simple question, maybe Cole has a point. "Have you ever tried... you know ... doing ... *it* ... at altitude?"

Sam's eyebrows shoot up, but he says nothing.

Instead of Cole, I'm suddenly imagining being locked in a very cramped space with Sam, and it's as if he can see straight into my oxygen-starved brain.

His eyes narrow. "*It*? What exactly are you asking me?"

Oh, Lord. My brain is shredded, on the rampage, tearing off clothes, running up the aisle of the airplane, yelling, "Chase me!" I do my best to look serious, but it's impossible not to think about what it might be like to have sex with the Rock on this plane. For someone scared of heights that would be quite the achievement...But this is just a harmless question. Research.

His smile broadens. "Go ahead. You can ask me anything."

"You know, the Mile High Club…" I can feel the blood coursing to my cheeks and it feels as if his eyes can see right inside my head. I swallow and lick my lips because my mouth has dried up. There's no harm in asking the question. It doesn't honestly matter what he thinks of me because I'll never see him again. I take a deep breath and ask, "*Haveyoueverhadsexinanairplane*?"

2

"Are you always so forward?" He's looking at me like I asked for his dick measurement.

I knock my tray, the empty plastic beaker slides toward the edge of the table, and Sam catches it. Again.

I flash him a look. "I was only asking! For a friend. I wasn't...You can't think... You don't seriously imagine I was propositioning *you*?"

"Weren't you?"

"I was not!" I bite my lip.

"Good because the answer would've been, shit no."

Shit, no? Shit no to having sex with me or shit no to having ever had sex at altitude? And why the shit anyhow? What's wrong with a simple no thank you?

"Listen, buddy, I was *not* asking if you'd like to have"—My voice has risen in tenor, so I dip my head and lower my voice—"sex with *me*, I was just asking the question in general. Like is the Mile High Club really a thing or not? What do you think?"

He stares at my mouth. "I think you may have had one too many drinks."

"You're taking this all the wrong way!"

"And there's a right way to take this? Call me old-fashioned, but to my mind sex and toilets, especially on planes, don't go well together unless you're desperate. Is that the problem? Has it been a long time?"

"No! God, no! I'm not desperate!"

"First of all, there's the awful smell," he continues, and his nostrils flare as if *I* smell bad. "Secondly, there's the cramped space which judging from your previous comments—"

"I was *not* asking you to *do* anything with me, let alone in the lavatory!"

"And then there are those tacky surfaces... ugh."

"I don't want to have sex with you!" I snap.

He's not listening. He's off on a flight path of his own. "I may look a little rough around the edges to you, but I do have some standards, Princess. Sex in toilets. Not my jam."

Someone clears their throat.

I look around.

Great, we have an audience. Mushroom Man is awake, mouth still gaping. He wipes his wet lips with the back of his hand ... and smiles warmly at me.

"Don't even!" I snarl. Facing the front, I cross my arms and close my eyes.

"Sex and showers on the other hand..." Sam's is still flying.

"Shut up, will you! Just shut up!"

"I didn't say a word," mumbles Mushroom.

"I wouldn't worry, mate," says Sam. "Noelle here has got it covered. Quite the conversationalist."

I want to curl up in a ball, only that's not possible in these seats. I screw my eyes tighter and clench my fists in my armpits. Get me out of here!

Thankfully, neither of the men says another word. I'm drained emotionally and physically. The unpleasant conversation with Sam runs on repeat in my head. Next to the party in my head is Cole who started this whole damn downward spiral.

♡♡♡

"So impatient, Noelle. I can't promote you just because we're sleeping together." Cole undoes a button on my cream silk blouse, and I do it up again.

I am sitting on his knee, feeling flustered and uncomfortably aware his mind is on other things. "Of course not, but I expected to get the Account Director role because you gave me the impression I was ready for it!" I was so ready. So ready, I'd already organized the layout of my new workspace. I'm beyond shocked Cole is still pondering this decision. "What's the problem with promoting me now?"

"Okay. One problem is that you're ... risk averse." He cocks his head.

"You say that like it's a bad thing."

"Babe, it is in our line of work... We have to be original. Willing to take risks." He pauses. "You need to think outside the box a little more. Be less conventional. Some of the guys feel you're too stand-offish and not really a team player."

A breath whistles out of me. "Okay, you told me not to get too pally with anyone here in the office."

He twists his mouth from side to side. "The words 'pushy and highly strung'" — he makes air quotes, which I hate— "have been bandied around."

"What? That's so out of order! If I were a man, I would no doubt be praised for being direct and to the point, and not afraid of speaking my mind. Any more dirt to throw at me?"

"Hey, don't shoot the messenger. But they might have also mentioned you being a bit uncooperative and uptight, but we can soon put a stop to that sort of idle gossip." Smiling, he starts trying to undo my buttons again.

I slap his hands away. "Stop it. I can't believe this. It's a total character assassination and you're finding this amusing. I am not here merely for your entertainment. I tried the cooperating thing, but then nothing ever gets achieved and you weren't happy with that situation either."

"I'm happy enough now." He starts loosening his tie. "So how cooperative are you feeling now?"

On a scale of one to ten, about minus ten. "Not now, Cole. Please!" He's so inappropriate. The way he's looking at me makes me grind my teeth. "We are *not* having sex in your office, right before a board meeting."

He runs a hand up my leg and I push it away. "Aren't we? I have to agree with the guys about some of the stuff they said. You could be more open-minded, especially when it comes to some important matters." His hand has returned. He rakes up my skirt. "You are inclined to be a little stiff."

Pow! I shoot upwards, wrenching myself out of his hands. "*Stiff!*"

"Okay, vanilla."

"*Vanilla*! Like that's any better! Cole, this promotion is important to me. I have worked damn hard to get where I am without having to use my family name. We have more important things to think about other than sex right now. We're about to go into a board meeting in which I was hoping you were going to announce me as the new Account Director. I do not want to look all … ruffled!"

He sighs like he has the weight of the world on his shoulders. He leans back in his chair. "Fine. I wonder if Vanessa Belmonte from HR would—"

"Go screw her if that's what you really want!" I turn and rush toward the door, but Cole slaps a hand on the door preventing me.

He kisses my neck. "Hey." Then he turns me around to face him. He is so handsome. So handsome and privileged and God damn *entitled*. He clasps my cheek in his hand. "Don't take everything so personally. But honey, I've decided to leave making any promotion announcements until the new year. Be patient … and perhaps you can inspire me over Christmas."

Patient is not really in my vocabulary. And I can't quite believe I've put up with Cole's bullshit for quite so long. I push him away. "Inspire you? You know what. Go inspire yourself over Christmas! I hope Santa brings you a toy to play with because I am done," I'd said, slapping his hands aside as I stalked out of his office.

I open my eyes, disoriented, heart pumping. No Cole here, thankfully. Just the airplane engines humming. Oh God, I'm still stuck in purgatory in mid-air and even worse, I'm slouched against Sam, my cheek on his shoulder. Cringing, I look up to find a grey pair of pupils inches from mine. Such long eyelashes. Such a waste on a man.

"Sorry!" I croak, sitting up hastily and surreptitiously wiping my mouth. Gawd. I have literally drooled all over him. Is there no end to my humiliation?

"No sweat," says Sam. Though there may be a puddle of dribble on his cashmere. "Feel better after sleeping it off?"

Looking at him, a piece of advice Lara once gave me pops into my head: good-looking does not equate to good. No, in Sam Devine's case good-looking equates to bad news. I don't merit him with an answer.

The air crew bring breakfast trays around and we eat in silence. I nurse my hangover and wounded pride. Both are in a very sorry state.

And I'm not sure how much longer I can endure being trapped in a flying coffin.

The air stewardess tries to sail past. I wave an arm and holler. "Excuse me, how much longer?"

She hesitates. "About forty-five minutes. Everything okay?"

"What does it look like?" I mutter slumping back in my seat again. "Fanfuckingtastic."

"What about you, sir, can I get you anything? At all?"

I have to admit, my nose is knocked ever so slightly out of joint because, although I may have literally salivated on Mr Devine, so far I haven't raised much more than a smirk from him and this flimflam is getting the full works: he is beaming like he's on a Hollywood red carpet. "I wouldn't mind a refill of water," says Sam. "Feeling slightly dry-mouthed. What about you, Noelle? Dry-mouthed?"

Asshole. New Zealand asshole.

"Coming right up, sir!" singsongs the air hostess.

God, if she gets any more sycophantic my breakfast is going to come right up all over the pair of them.

3

I've never been so happy to see the back of someone as I am to see the back of Sam Devine striding out of the airport with Nothing-to-Declare (other than the fact he's another arrogant self-absorbed moron), while I'm still waiting for my additional luggage.

I hire a car. It should take me about six hours to drive to Queenstown. Lara had offered to come and pick me up, which is just the sort of crazy thing she'd do a couple of days before her own wedding, however, I insist on driving myself. After a distressing end to my working year, not to mention the plane trip from hell, I need time to adjust.

I get halfway to Queenstown when I see signs for a spa and the enchanting blue of Lake Tekapo. I pull the car up on the side of the road. It looks like the perfect restorative. The scenery is breathtaking.

I book myself in for the night, and also book a Day Spa for the next day which includes full body massage, facial, a manicure and pedicure. I reckon after the flight from hell, I deserve some serious pampering. I ring Lara and plead jet lag and some bug I possibly caught on the plane. I promise to be on my way again as soon as I feel able.

Lara sounds only slightly disappointed. "No worries. You'll miss all the fun I planned, and I was so looking forward to you meeting the other bridesmaids." I'm sort of disappointed she doesn't sound more distraught.

"Me too, Lara, but I'll have plenty of time to get to know them at the wedding."

"I'm expecting you to show these Kiwi girls how to party."

"I will. I'm looking forward to it. I'll be there soon enough."

"Okay, you do sound a bit croaky, and I don't want to catch anything before the big day."

I laugh and disconnect.

Something feels dislodged, like there are a few loose nuts and bolts rattling around inside me. I need my mojo restoring. The last thing I want to do is go off the rails in front of Lara and all her wedding guests. But I honestly feel as if I am teetering on the brink of something huge...like a nervous breakdown.

Lying on my bed, I make my next duty call and phone my parents to let them know I've arrived.

"That's good to hear," says my mother. "Arrived where?" No-one has perfected condescension like her. Perhaps it's the French accent.

I pull a face, thankful she cannot see it. "New Zealand. For Lara's wedding."

"New Zealand! Lara?"

I roll my eyes. She never listens to me.

"Yes, Lara Wiseman," I say.

There's a choking sound. It seems I've finally got her attention. "*Zut alors!* That *Larr-rrah!* Where did you say you were?" Now she's rolling her Rs and making guttural noises.

"On my way to Queenstown, New Zealand."

"*C'est impossible! Non,* Noelle! What are you thinking, *imbécile!* The two of you parted company years ago. You've nothing in common with that girl."

Mama never did approve of my friendship with Lara. You could see it in the way her expression hardened at the sight of Lara's outfits, but her distaste had really calcified when Lara's family lost everything after her father was imprisoned for fraud. Both my parents made no bones about the fact they wanted me to cut ties. I hadn't done that while we were at school, but nor had I encouraged Lara to keep in touch afterwards. Life is too short and she is the best friend I've ever had. I miss her. And Lord knows, right now I could do with a friend.

"We lost touch, but not entirely. She asked me to be her maid-of-honor, and we always promised one another—"

"I cannot believe you would consider such a thing! Maid-of-honor indeed, more like made-of-trash. Wake up! She's trying to sink her claws into you again."

"That's a little extreme."

"As is you flying to New Zealand to keep her happy because of some ridiculous childhood promise. You should be home for Christmas. I'd no idea—"

"You did because I told you about this when we last spoke. You didn't seem concerned about it then." There's silence. "Anyway, too bad. I'm already here."

"Mon dieu!" She puffs out an exasperated breath. "Wait until your father hears. Wait until Amelie hears. They'll both have something to say about this."

Somehow, I doubt it. If he wasn't told about my absence, he'd probably not even notice, and my sister Amelie is far too busy with her acting career to even notice I'm not there. "I'll call you all on Christmas Day."

"And when shall I tell your father to expect you back here?"

"I'm not sure. I'm staying in New Zealand for a couple of weeks. I've agreed to house-sit for Lara while she's away on honeymoon."

"See, there you go. She's already has you running around after her doing favors again."

"No, she's doing me the favor. I *want* to be here."

"Well, say hello to the donut and don't say I didn't warn you it'll end in disaster." She ends the call and I'm left staring in frustration and mounting anger at my cellphone.

So much for motherly love.

I stalk out of the hotel and into town.

I had forgotten that she used to call Lara the Donut. My mother can be harsh. Admittedly, Lara and I had been somewhat obsessed with donuts as kids. When did *I* last have one? I feel like eating one now, anything to sweeten the bitter taste in my mouth. I lick my lips imagining tasting the cinnamon sugar that had once made me so deliriously happy. Or had I been addicted to Lara? She'd always been such a free spirit and part of me had always envied that. Plus her mother wasn't quite such an unconscionable bitch. I'd take her criminal father over my mother any day.

I go in hunt of donuts and my efforts are rewarded. In a supermarket, I buy a box of four. Returning to my room, I eat three before feeling sick and miserable. I hope this New Zealand trip isn't going to be one big horrible mistake. Maybe I should have stayed in the States and worked on my relationship with Cole.

Absence makes the heart grow fonder, doesn't it? Maybe he needs a bit more of a reminder of what he's missing and that doesn't mean me eating donuts. I want Cole begging for me to take that promotion. I want him begging me to come back to him. I change into my bikini and take a couple of photos of me by the hotel swimming pool. I post them to Instagram. I need to use this wedding to do some marketing of my own. Make Cole realize I'm not 'risk averse' or 'standoffish' or 'stiff' or 'vanilla' or any of the other words he called me.

It may be the quietest Christmas ever, but I need to make him think I'm having a the time of my life. The photo of me by the pool looks okay, but it's not exactly saying 'glamorous'. I need to up my game. Meanwhile, I have a post-sugar crash to deal with.

♡♡♡

I don't arrive in Queenstown until the evening before the wedding and even then I'm late, accidentally (on purpose) missing dinner with her nearest and dearest. I don't know why I procrastinate. I'm so nervous my palms are sweating. My usual reserves of confidence have evaporated with the heat.

Lara texts me her home address which is beyond Queenstown on the Te Araroa Bypass. We squeal like the giddy schoolgirls we once were, when we see one another.

"Nollie, you made it!" yells Lara.

"Lara, look the heck at you!" I scream back.

Holding onto her arms, I take a step back to admire her. She's looking amazing. I can't stop checking out the toned muscles in her arm and her athletic body. What has happened to Lara the Donut? It's incredible. And surprisingly, her house on the lake is incredible too.

Lara and Shaun live in a barn they've converted and restored themselves and there's not a sheep in sight. Well maybe a small huddle a few hills away... Their land has direct frontage onto a lake — Lake Wakatipu, Lara informs me proudly — and they have their own private jetty and boatshed. Beyond the lake, mountains jigsaw across the blue velvet sky. It's stunning. Truly majestic. Not much in the way of civilization around here, but Lara reassures me Queenstown is the adventure capital of the world — I'm not entirely sure her idea of an adventure and mine reconcile, but still, this place makes a nice change from my usual hustle and bustle of the city.

"Is he here?"

She shakes her head. "Shaun is kind of traditional. We're not seeing each other the day before the wedding, but I've had my best friends to keep me company and they're here to meet you of course."

If *they're* her best friends, what does that make me? I try to swallow my pride as she introduces me to her bridesmaids—Gladys, Hana and Maia — who are waiting to meet me. They're friendly enough, but I can't help feeling there is a slight frostiness in the air between us, especially Gladys whose slightly bulbous unblinking eyes unsettle me even more. Maybe it's because the sun is setting and the temperature has dropped that I have the chills. Maybe it has nothing to do with the fact I feel judged: the maid-of-honor who has only just made an appearance. Did Gladys get demoted from the role?

We share a couple of glasses of sparkling wine, but I'm thankful when the clucking brood of bridesmaids eventually leave because it means alone time with Lara, and we have a load of catching up to do.

"Come on. It's still warm. Let's go and sit on the dick," says Lara.

"The dick?" I repeat, giggling.

"The deck," she says rolling her eyes.

"You're sounding like such a Kiwi these days," I tease.

"I know. I feel a part of this place already. I love it here," she sighs.

We take our drinks outside and before long it's like the good old days: chatting under the stars and gossiping like teenagers.

"Was I imagining it, or have I done something to put Gladys's nose out of joint?" I ask.

"Don't sweat. Gladys is a bit upset she's been demoted to head bridesmaid and is no longer maid-of-honor, that's all."

"No longer?"

"When you said you couldn't come because of work, I asked her, and then had to un-ask her when you changed your mind. But I'm very glad you did! She's cool with it. It really doesn't matter." She grabs my hand and squeezes. "Once I explained our childhood promise to be each other's maid-of-honor, Gladys was cool with everything."

Cool being the operative word.

"Can you believe I'm getting married? I honestly thought it would be you to fall first, but I can still be your matron-of-honor when you eventually get around to tying the knot."

"Ha! Well, don't hold your breath. That's not happening any time soon and with my luck with men—"

"Because you're all about your career these days!" She smiles. "So, how is work?"

Ugh. I'd rather not think about it, but if anyone can set me right, it's Lara. I spill the tea on Cole. It's funny how we slip back into our friendship as easily as putting on a comfortable—slightly threadbare—but no less favorite pair of jeans. I also recount the humiliation on the plane seated between the Rock and the Mushroom.

Lara's raucous laughter peels through the valley loud enough to wake distant neighbors and start an avalanche, but when she tells me about Shaun, her voice takes on this hushed reverent tone. My heart swells and I banish any misgivings. I can't wait to meet him. I can't help but be happy for her. We're teenagers again, reminiscing, filling the gaps in each other's recent past history and she's so obviously in love, I couldn't be anything but thrilled.

We're both in a pajamas on our way to bed when Lara hugs me hard. "One day you'll find the one for you, Nol."

"Sure. I wish you were still in America. It seemed so much easier when we had each other's back. We have to work out a way to see each other more than once every five years in future."

"I know! I miss this," she replies, "but don't worry, I have a plan."

"Oh swell. I'd forgotten you and your schemes. Who does it involve this time?"

"Did I mention how gorgeous the best man is and that he spends half his life California?" She sits down on the end of my bed.

I know Lara's taste in men, but I humor her, after all it is the night before her wedding. "On the scale of hot, how hot is he?"

"Inferno. Hellishly hot. And he's going to fall head-over-heels in love with you because you are exactly his type, and then we are going to live in each other's pockets for the rest of our lives."

"Ha! Oh yeah, sounds like the perfect solution apart from the fact that I live in America and you're here in New Zealand and he's a Kiwi! I mean, no offense, I'm sure Shaun is lovely and all that, but I told you about that rude dude on the plane. I think I'll stick with Americans, thank you very much."

"What like *Cole*? Cos he doesn't sound like a total douche."

"You're going to be in so much trouble with Sam, you might as well kiss any Christmas peace of mind goodbye."

"Sam? Sam? The dude on the plane was called Sam!"

She laughs. "Just imagine if it was the same guy."

"Thank you, but I'd rather not have nightmares tonight."

Lara heads for the door. "I need to get some beauty sleep. You have sweet dreams. Whatever's going on, you'll be fine, Noelle. You always are."

Am I though? I wish I had her confidence. My foundations seem to have been shaken recently.

After we say our goodnights, I struggle to fall asleep sifting through memories of the conversation on the plane with Sam, searching for any signs that he could have known who I was talking about or could have been going to a wedding. There'd been nothing. It couldn't possibly be the same Sam. There must be a million Sams in New Zealand, but nevertheless, my pulse is now beating erratically, and I am horribly awake.

4

It's true, perhaps I have become uptight, I think as I shy away from my outfit.

"What's wrong?" asks Gladys eyeballing me.

"Nothing. Nothing at all. I just wondered who robbed Santa's grotto?"

"Santa's grotto? What the hell?"

"I'm joking, Gladys!" I say, although I'm really really not.

I grit my teeth and smile because I am not going to be the one to shatter Lara's happiness and admit that although the setting is sublime, the inside of the wedding venue looks like a festive sleigh crash. When will Lara learn that less is more? In fact, in this case, *nothing* would be more.

"Aren't I lucky Maia's a florist. She's spent hours this morning doing these flower arrangements, and she's done such an awesome job," says Lara right behind me.

Oops. I spin around.

She looks strained. Clearly she heard every word I just said.

"I wanted everything to look Christmassy as well as bridal. I think it looks fine, don't you, Gladys?"

"Divine!"

Ha. That word again. *Divine* conjures up nightmares of stuntmen and a near-death experience and a taste of bile. Pinpricks of sweat break out across my brow. But I'm determined to put on a dazzling show of steadfast loyalty to my bestie. "This place looks stunning ... It's unique. I've never seen anything like it. You are so lucky." If she'd invited all of Santa's elves and even the hobbits from Hobbiton, I'd suck it up and love it. This is Lara's day. She must be made to feel like a queen. Even if that's Queen of Tinseltown.

We're ushered into a large bedroom suite where Lara's wedding dress hangs from the picture rail.

"Wow!" I am again stunned. It's not so much a meringue as a full on New Zealand pavlova which I hear is their national dish, so I guess she's taken that to heart. "It's A-MAZ-ING!" Holy cows and all their udders.

I should have guessed what the order of the day would be from the moment Gladys handed me what can only be described as my own pantomime costume first thing this morning. "What the heck is this?" I asked.

There'd been silence. You could have heard a pin drop.

"It's your dress," said Maia.

"But it's ... it's absolutely...ab..." My eyes caught Lara's. I suddenly felt like I was hanging from a cliff by my fingernails.

"A bit green?" said Lara, looking desperately worried.

"It's *mermaid* green," Gladys had said, as if that made it any better. It may actually look half decent on her with her olive coloring.

"No, it's...it's..." I searched frantically for a fitting word. "*Spectacular*. I was going to say absolutely *spectacular!*" I wasn't kidding; nor was I fooling anyone. The dress is so hideous it's likely to stop traffic. It is more than green and the only thing festive about it is that I am going to resemble a fir tree. With my pale skin it's already making me feel bilious. How fitting. At least the material color will match my complexion.

"We chose them before I knew you were coming," whispered Lara. "I know green is not your favorite color, but..." Lara's lower lip trembled, and I felt bad. She knows I don't wear green. Apart from the fact it looks awful on me, green is unlucky. Okay, I'm a little superstitious about these things, but today I'm going to have to put up and shut up.

"But not this green! It is a gorgeous green. A glorious green! Besides, I love green these days." I force a smile. "Let's have another glass of champagne to toast the bride. Here's to Lara!"

The bridesmaids seem happy to comply. My smile feels crusty as I plug my glass of champagne. We always used to joke about what a fashion assassin Lara was, but I guess now is not the occasion. Nothing is going to dent my enthusiasm, not even a gaping cowl neckline and knowledge that anyone taller than me will have a bird's-eye view of my cleavage — or total lack of.

"We're all look amazing," says Gladys, handing me a tiara and some red bauble earrings. *Red bauble earrings.* No shit.

"We're definitely going to cause a sensation," I say, attaching the red baubles to my earlobes with a smile befitting an angel on top of a Christmas tree. All I need is fairy lights and I'll be ready to light up the town.

I will not weep. I will not throw a tantrum. I will stick my smile as firmly in place as Hana, our very own hairdresser, who is now fixing the bejeweled tiaras to our tresses. There are a multitude of pins. And she really goes to town with the loops and hoops. And the hairspray.

Mustn't stand too close to any live flames, I think, pressing my lips firmly together. I am not going to pass judgment on Hana or Maia or Gladys or Lara. I am not going to mess up this special day with stupid snide comments like my mother would. Nor am I going to be that loud embarrassing American like my father. I am going to be serene. As silent as a small Swiss fir tree.

Ready for action, we parade from our dressing room like a forest on the move — imagine all the grace of Macbeth's Dunsinane on the march behind the bride.

As we step outside, the sound of stringed classical music, a little strangled on some notes, floats toward us. I do my best to look demure, soft and floaty, rather than needly and green. It's not as easy as it sounds. It's hot as an oven outside, and I think I may be shedding needles.

We process toward the small stone chapel beside the lake. As we walk up the aisle between the seats, I focus on the cool shimmering water beyond the red-ribboned arch rather than the perspiration gathering in my hairline.

No negative thoughts. I'm here to celebrate Lara's love and future happiness.

The mountains really are magnificent, and Lara looks blissfully happy on the dais beside her groom. Shaun is short and dark, and really rather cute. The way he looks at Lara as if she is the most perfect woman he's every laid eyes on actually makes me forget everything else, and my heart swells for them and my eyes fill with tears. This is what love looks like. I blink my tears away as Lara hands me her bouquet to look after. I take my place in the second row behind immediate family. And scan the congregation.

For the first time I set eyes on the best man, and suddenly all fingers and thumbs, I drop the bouquet. *No.*

No, no, no.

It is Sam.

My breath catches in my throat and I blink fiercely. But he doesn't disappear. It is my Sam. Not *my* Sam, but THAT Sam. Sam Devine.

How is this even possible? What are the chances? I'd convinced myself it'd be too much of a coincidence, but it's not. It's really him. I crouch to retrieve the flowers and take a moment to steady my breathing. Hot is not a fitting word for today; this is hell on Earth, and some how I have to rise above it all...

I steady myself on the chair, before, acknowledging I can't stay down here forever. I begin to rise.

I don't get far before the chair in front of me lifts and I practically scalp myself. *What the hell?* Bent double, I grope blindly with my hands. Oh Lord, somehow my tiara and hair arrangement have become entangled with the seat decoration which adorns the back of the chair in front of me. Twisting painfully, I glance sideways along the line of chairs and see bunches of red tinsel and silver bells. *Hells bells! I can't spend the entire service down here.* Desperately, I attempt to free myself.

"Hold still!" hisses Gladzilla next to me.

I spend the next ten minutes of the ceremony on my knees, Gladys no doubt earning her celestial payback for not being made maid-of-honor, mercilessly yanking my hair until my eyes water and she finally frees me.

I emerge at the end of the first hymn, my face no doubt a nice shade of volcanic red.

"Thank you," I mumble to Gladys.

She hands me a service sheet, and for the first time since I've met her, she looks truly delighted. "Happy to be of assistance," she says slipping a pen knife back into her clutch bag.

What kind of woman takes a pen knife to a wedding?

I suppose I should feel lucky she didn't slit my throat.

Apprehensively I raise a hand to my tender scalp. It feels like a bird has nested and taken a dump on top of my head. There's definitely some additional millinery still attached.

I make the fatal mistake of looking toward the groomsmen and Sam winks at me.

I look beyond him. The lake is serene. The mountains are still magnificent. The weather is glorious. Love is in the air...

♡♡♡

"Nice tiara," says Sam.

"Nice tux," I mutter, clutching Lara's wedding bouquet tighter — it's either that or bat him around the back of the head with it, and I've already caused spectacle enough. The wedding ceremony has already been and gone in a blur of embarrassment.

"Who'd have thought we'd meet again quite so soon, hey?" says Sam.

Understatement of the year. "Yes, quite the surprise."

We're stuck in human traffic. Lara and Shaun are stopping to greet their guests. My mind reels back to everything I may or may not have said on the plane. I suspect I said something about Lara having abominable taste in men. Could they not process along this aisle a little bit faster?

"So Lara was the best friend you were speaking about. On the plane?" says Sam leaning toward me and speaking out of the corner of his mouth.

"Mmmhmm." As if he didn't know already.

"And has the wedding lived up to your expectations?"

I grit my teeth. God give me strength, or a crowbar, anything to get me out of this hideous situation. "It's been lovely so far."

"Mmm. My favorite moment was right at the beginning. For a while there, I wondered if you were deliberately sabotaging things. You almost stole the bride's limelight."

I glance his way before I can stop myself. He's grinning like a loon. I suppose I should be happy he doesn't think I did it on purpose.

Sam's eyes stray to the top of my head. "You're hair is awesome by the way. Very original."

If only looks could really kill.

I turn to face the bride again. We're almost at the end of the aisle. I will her to stop greeting family and friends so effusively and extensively and get the hell on with things. "Lara looks radiant," I say.

"You too. Think you might have caught the sun," says Sam.

Oh great. I have also forgotten to put on any suncream and with my fair skin, that doesn't bode well.

"Will you be drinking champagne at all today?" Sam asks, reaching for two glasses from a nearby waiter.

I can't deal with this any more. I snatch the glass out of his hands, turn on my heel and almost run to the Ladies Powder Room. I am not going to let him ruin my day. It does kind of put me off Shaun if he is friends with such a prize jerk.

I check myself in the mirror. *Holy shit.* I look a hot mess. I stand in front of the air conditioning unit trying to cool down. Then it takes me half an hour to flatten my frizz and redo my make-up.

On the way back outside, I check out the seating plan. Of course. I'm seated next to Sam Devine. That's just what I need.

By the time I find Lara, the sun is starting to soften, thankfully, and I take some time to appreciate the moment and breathe in the golden light. This is how I'm going to be for the rest of the evening. I shall glow and be golden and not break into a cold sweat sitting next to Sam, damn the man.

Everyone is chatting and drinking. "Congratulations, Mrs Mann! I'm so incredibly thrilled for you." I pull Lara into a warm embrace.

"Can you believe it? Mrs Mann!" she says. "Wait. You haven't met Shaun officially yet. Shaun, come meet Noelle."

Shaun takes my hands in his. "I've heard so much about you." He gives me a strange look. A suspicious look. Before pulling me into a tight bearhug.

"Be careful. You might crush this awesome dress," I say trying to laugh it off.

Shaun has a great rumbling laugh and twinkling eyes and it's easy to see why Lara is so smitten.

"Congratulations both of you! What a wonderful ceremony!" I say.

"Plenty more fun to come."

"We've been remiss. We haven't introduced Noelle to Sam yet either," says Lara.

"No need. We met already," I say a bit to hastily. There's a beat of silence. "Moments ago, after the ceremony, we met. And I'll meet him again soon enough as I'm sitting next to him at dinner."

"I'll go find him," says Shaun.

I want to run and hide in a closet, but I'm hemmed in being introduced to Lara's friends and neighbors. My eyes keep straying across the lawn to where Sam and Shaun are talking rather animatedly. At one point, I catch Sam's eyes and he hastily turns his back to me. Like that isn't suspect. Perhaps he imagines I can lip read.

Somewhere a bell tinkles ominously. Crap. Time for dinner. Time to take our seats. Unceremoniously, I drain my glass of champagne.

The top table is long and rectangular decorated with a strip of gold cloth and more festive tinselly goodness. I give it all a wide birth.

Heading for my allotted place, I rehearse polite innocuous lines to say to Sam. But I'm surprised to see he's heading for the other end of the table.

"Hi, I'm Greg," says a voice beside me. "One of the groomsmen. I hope you don't mind I've been switched."

"Oh. Not at all." As I look up, he tilts his head and inspects me.

"You really remind me of someone — "

"Noelle Foley?" says another familiar voice in my ear. "Well, goddamn, I'll be damned!"

Undoubtedly.

I never find out who I remind Greg of because I am face-to-face with Lara's father, Bill. He's aged. He looks grizzled. "I didn't know ... I had no idea...you—"

"Were out of jail?" He leans forward, clamps a hand on my shoulder and squeezes. "Six months ago. Great to have escaped."

"Great," I whimper.

5

Sometimes life seems, well, just a little unfair. And the adage, money does not buy you happiness, a jarring truth. My trip to New Zealand is meant to be a happy one, a reprieve from the messy situation at work and a chance to reunite with Lara. It should be the opportunity to figure out exactly what I'm going to do with my life. Right at that moment, I wish I could escape too. I hoped to recharge my batteries. It was meant to be a reprieve from Cole and my family, and an opportunity to figure out exactly what I'm going to do with my future. Instead, I find myself flagging, sinking lower and lower into my seat as Bill, laughing, regales me with anecdotes about playing golf with my father and the lengths Dad would go to just to ensure he won. "You Foleys certainly like to take things to extremes, don't you?"

"Do we?"

"Well, I was surprised to hear you'd come all this way," says Bill," seeing as you haven't exactly kept in touch with Lara." He frowns. "Not heard from your father either since I was put behind bars…I guess he was too busy to answer my calls."

"If it's any consolation, he's too busy to answer my calls too," I say, attempting to make light of it, "and I wouldn't have missed this for the world."

Bill nods ruminatively. "You don't say."

I get the distinct impression he can see through my distorted version of the truth and is another person who would rather be seated elsewhere.

While Bill and Greg talk across me about sport, I study the menu. Griddled groper salad with chili, lychee, lime and apple. What in hell's name is groper? It sounds indecent. Followed by pistachio-crusted lamb rump, plum and redcurrant jus, kumara and potato gratin. I have no idea what kumara is either. Dessert is *petit fours*. I suppose I should be happy we're not eating roast turkey just to keep with the Christmassy theme.

So that's the menu studied. What next? Could this wedding get any more awkward? Across the far side of the table, Sam is looking incredibly relaxed, laughing uproariously at whatever Gladys is telling him. He glances over and our eyes catch. Hastily, I act like there's nothing more fascinating than rugby —I'm the biggest fan!— not that I've ever watched a game. It's not long before my attention wanders off again.

Much as I love Lara and want to be loyal, this is without doubt the most uncomfortable and outlandish and bizarre wedding I've ever attended. Maia has knocked herself out with the decorations — possibly literally. There is a tinseled pole slap bang in the center of the room. I stare at it, trying to figure out what purpose it could possibly serve, before concluding that my and Lara's tastes are still poles apart. Smiling at my own little joke, I happen to lock eyes with Sam again. I throw my head back in feigned laughter, clutching hold of Greg's arm. "That's hilarious!"

Greg and Bill look at me as if I'm an idiot.

"They were mullered," says Greg.

"Okay, I guess more funny-peculiar than funny-haha," I say.

After that, drinking seems to be the obvious solution.

Keeping my head down, smiling occasionally, I pretend I'm fully engaged in the wedding table conversation, until someone taps a glass.

"Here goes," says Bill, getting to his feet. He makes a great speech which has Lara in tears. He's brutally frank about missing the best years of his daughter's life because he was imprisoned. "When she had it tough in her teenage years, she could have lost her way, but she didn't. She was lucky enough to have great school friends like Noelle here, to help see her through." He squeezes my shoulder and I tear up too. "Despite all the hurdles life has thrown at these girls, and some dubious role models as parents,"—there is muffled laughter—"Lara has grown into a daughter I couldn't be more proud of. Independent, compassionate, caring, determined..."

I somehow doubt my parents would be so effusive in their praise. What sort of a person does that make me? A lesser one than Lara, that's for sure.

Bill sits down to enthusiastic applause.

"Thank you for your kind words," I say. "That was a great speech."

"Have you prepared a few words? You know Lara better than anyone and it seems a bit unfair to let us men do all the talking."

"I suppose I could."

The best man's speech is announced, and Sam gets to his feet. The knot in my stomach tightens. He's an action man; part of me hopes his speech will be terrible. I'm woefully disappointed.

"As a stuntman I get asked to do a lot of crazy things," he says, his eyes locked onto me. Everyone is smiling, except me, because I'm rigid with anxiety, my stomach bottoming out, aware of heads swiveling to look in my direction to find out what he's staring at. "Hell, on the flight over the woman sitting next to me asked if I'd joined the mile-high club, and I don't think she was talking about walking on the wings." Amid the laughter, he keeps on looking at me and my hand tightens around the stem of my glass.

"I won't deny I get an adrenalin buzz from a challenge," he continues. "But I know when to say no. I couldn't survive in this business if I didn't calculate the risks versus the rewards."

I don't think he's calculated the risks of taking jabs at me in his speech, like the risk of having a champagne bottle cracked over his head.

"Before I became a stuntman, I studied engineering. The reason

I'm still alive is because every stunt and every rig is the opposite of reckless. It's calculated to the nth degree. I always choose the safest option."

Finally, he breaks our staring competition and looks at Shaun and Lara.

"When Shaun first told me he'd proposed to Lara, they'd only been dating a couple of weeks. I thought it was just a stupid stunt, and a reckless one at that. But how wrong could I have been? I've got to know Lara since, and I've seen how great these two are together. This marriage is like the best gig, because Lara and Shaun are the ultimate combination. They'll challenge and excite each other every day, but they'll also be each other's safety net." He raises his glass. "Please be upstanding and toast the bride and groom. May your married lives be full of fun and excitement, thrills without spills, and may you never let each other fall."

There's lots of clapping and cheering. Along with everyone else, I toast the bride and groom before I beckon a passing waiter to refill my glass. When everyone else sits, I remain standing.

"As Lara, sorry, Lara's oldest friend here, I'd like to say a few words too, please!" I'm pretty good at raising my voice, especially after a couple of drinks. Maybe I do have some of my father's genes.

The room quietens.

"Bill here asked if I was going to say something tonight. He said I couldn't let the men do all the talking. How true! And when do I ever have nothing to say, Lara?"

She laughs.

"Unfortunately, or should I say *fortunately* for all of you, I haven't prepared anything, so I'll keep this short. I want to reiterate, Shaun, you couldn't find a better partner and friend than Lara. She's loyal and loving and caring and definitely the kindest person I know." I look at Lara, tears welling in my eyes. Hell. "Lara has strong values. And knowing what to value in life can sometimes be confusing." My voice cracks for no reason, so I take a slurp of wine. "Seeing Lara again after so many years, too many years, has reminded me just how much I value our friendship, no matter how far apart we are. I love that she always embraces life. Without fail. She makes the most of opportunities and reminds the rest of us girls that we have glass ceilings to smash, and that we have to get out and live life to the full." Oh Lord, I'm sounding choked. I need to wrap this up. "And boy Lara's chosen well in Shaun." I glance at Sam, who's leaning back in his chair staring at the ceiling as if I'm putting him to sleep. "Life should not be dull. It should be an adventure. We could all do with some of that. And sometimes it's worth taking risks in life, otherwise we'll never know what could be possible..."

Out of the corner of my eye, I see Sam link his hands behind his head, clearly bored. "Anyway, what I'm trying to say is keep living life to the full, and everyone else, please raise a glass to toast Lara and Shaun's latest grand adventure—married life!"

I neck my drink and sit down. Oh God, that was awful. I want to crawl under the table with embarrassment.

Bill squeezes my shoulder. "You know, Noelle, if I were thirty years younger, I'd be tempted to take a few risks..." He winks at me again.

6

"I apologize," says Sam.

I shrug, attempting to look more nonchalant than I feel. "The answer is still no. Definitely not."

Sam and I are standing together on the terrace, looking out at the lake, and I for one am trying to look like we are having a civilized and polite conversation rather than a heated argument over a dance.

"Listen, you're right and I apologize. I did sort of get the wrong first impression of you."

"Gosh, like that's original. Are you expecting me to thank you for insulting me every time you open your mouth."

The corner of his mouth lifts. "You kind of make yourself an easy target." He lifts his hands in surrender, when I glare at him. "But ... I acknowledge I haven't been altogether fair. I admit you weren't actually propositioning me on the plane, okay?"

"Wow-wee. It's a little late for an apology now you've given everyone here the impression I was chasing you for ...sex," I hiss.

"Fair enough. I don't particularly want to dance either, I'm just trying to keep Shaun and Lara happy."

I glare at him again. "And I'm not? There you go again making out I'm some sort of...of...selfish bitch. If you do not walk away very soon, you are in danger of having the contents of this glass tipped over your head and that would be a waste of good champagne."

He sighs. "Right. I'll let Lara and Shaun know neither of us want to do it."

I harrumph.

"Even though they specifically asked that we help get the party started." His mouth twists and he thrusts his hands in his pants' pockets. "Even though in your speech you sounded like you were very keen to grab any opportunity for adventure—"

"Stop right there." I turn and face him. "Funnily enough, dancing with you, does not feel like an opportunity or an adventure. It sounds more like a punishment."

His lips pucker, and I can tell the bastard is trying not to laugh. "Right. I'm probably overthinking this. Dancing in front of everyone would be a big deal...for you. Imagine if you missed a beat or God forbid, tripped over."

I smile through gritted teeth. "I'm not interested in sex or dancing or anything else for that matter with the likes of you, so you can keep your little life tips and ... and take your sorry ass and find someone else to humiliate!"

He bows and takes a step backwards. "Message received loud and clear. I'll go and tell Lara and Shaun that's a definite no."

"I'd appreciate that."

"What if I confess ... I was tempted by your not-a-proposition on the plane?"

A snort of laughter escapes me. "Yeah, right. You were not."

"Okay, I wasn't. Not until tonight, anyhow. Now I'm intrigued to know. Who were you asking for? Cole?"

I'm amazed he can remember my ex's name. Perhaps he was paying more attention to my drunken ramblings on the plane than I gave him credit for. "It really doesn't matter."

"My guess is maybe it was something he once suggested and you—"

"Could you just stop already?" I stare at him in disbelief, anger bubbling because he's a little too close to the bone.

"Am I getting warm?"

Just warm? "Not remotely." I narrow my eyes, raise my chin and fold my arms. I hate him and his casual manner. He makes me feel hot and twitchy.

Inside the winery, the band strike up and someone announces the bride and groom are about to hit the dance floor for their first dance.

"Excuse me. Perhaps I'll go and find someone else to dance with." I sweep past him feeling a little bit smug.

"Ladies and gentlemen, Mr and Mrs Mann," someone announces.

The music kicks off with Lara's favorite: Marvin Gaye's *Ain't no mountain high enough*.

Lara and Shaun's first dance is jaw-dropping, and now I get exactly why the pole is there. When they are not twirling around one another, they are twirling around the pole, now relieved of its tinsel. Lara and Shaun dance without inhibition, their love for one another seems to shine from every pore — it's unapologetic and shameless and magnificent. I wish I could be like that ... Instead, I feel like I spend my whole life feeling like an imposter — out of place and not good enough. Not good enough for my parents. Not good enough for Cole. And definitely not good enough for a friend like Lara.

Their dance ends in rapturous applause and raucous whistling. And then the dance floor is empty again, everyone else slightly reluctant follow suit.

Lara beckons me on the dance floor and I realize Sam has appeared right beside me.

"No worries. I'll go and let them know you'd rather not make an exhibition of yourself," says Sam.

As he strides across the dance floor toward Lara and Shaun, I rush after him. "Wait!" No way is he getting to announce I've chickened out. I'd much rather make my own excuses.

I skid to a stop in front of them. "About this dance with Sam," I begin.

Lara claps her hands gleefully. "You little star! I knew you'd come through, Noelle. I can't wait to see this. Watch out, Sam. She used to be quite the mover and groover at school."

Her reaction seems a mite overblown and I hesitate trying to figure out what she's quite so excited about. "I—"

"Thank you, thank you , thank you, both," says Lara. "This is the best wedding present ever. We've been begging Sam to dance for us for weeks. Finally, he said he'd do it, but only if you agreed to dance with him." She gives Sam a nudge. "I think he was depending on you saying no, but I knew you wouldn't let us down." She hugs me.

I glare at Sam over her shoulder, but he and Shaun are already strolling to the other side of the dance floor to talk to the band. I'm in a state of shock. "After your and Shaun's performance this is going to be—"

I'm interrupted by Shaun tapping the microphone and clearing his throat. "Family and friends, it's taken quite a bit of persuasion, but Mr Sam Devine has agreed to kick off the dancing for real tonight with one of his rare performances. You are in for a treat," says Shaun.

What does he mean by 'his very rare performances'? Why is there an excited buzz in the audience and a few cheers?

"All you have to do is follow Sam's lead," says Lara in my ear.

The skin on the back of my neck prickles. She gives my arm a squeeze and pushes me onto the dance floor. A raft of goosebumps travels up my spine and I spin around looking for an escape, but I'm trapped on the dance floor, the crowd pressing in on every side, the center of attention.

Why the hell is Lara looking so excited? What is going on?

"As most of you'll know, Sam spends most of his time working abroad for Hollywood these days," says Shaun. "He's a hard man to pin down at the best of times and seldom takes to the stage even when he's in town at his club, Devine Devils, so Lara and I could not be more thrilled that he's here with us tonight."

I am not thrilled. My throat is seizing up. I can hardly breathe. Despite it being hot in here, I feel icy cold beneath the spotlight.

What does Shaun mean, Sam seldom takes to the stage? What the hell sort of club is Devine Devils? What have I got myself into now?

"Put your hands together for the amazing, the incredible, the super talented Sam Devine and his partner-in-crime the plucky maid-of-honor, our one and only adventure-seeking Noelle Foley!"

Sam walks over and takes my hand. "Ever pole-danced?"

"What? No!"

"Never too late to learn," he says.

"It so—" The band starts up. *You can leave your hat on.* My eyes lock onto Sam's. *No, no. God, no, please!* This cannot be happening to me. A whimper escapes me as Sam does a couple of backward flips.

Baby, take off... Staring across at me, Sam slips out of his tuxedo and throws it. It hits me in the face. I'm little better than a mannequin, stiff with fear, inhaling the smell of him from his jacket... Slowly, more terrified than I have been in my life, I peek over the edge of his tuxedo.

No, no, no, no , no...

Sam mouths the words to the song and his hips begin to gyrate.

He's smiling this sexy grin with his come hither eyes...and I am going to murder him! *I'm going to murder—*

But faster than proverbial greased lightning Sam has slid across the dance floor and is behind me, his arms wrapping around me, breathing reassuring nonsense in my ear. *You can leave your...* He could be murmuring anything, *You can leave your thermals, ski jacket and snow boots on,* and this could not be any more torturous as he grinds behind me.

Pulling his tuxedo from my clenched fists, he throws it at a laughing woman in the crowd and from somewhere he has magicked a hat which he plonks on my head. It falls over my eyes as he swings me around to face him. Hands on my hips, he murmurs, "Baby, relax. Just dance. Forget I'm even here."

"Like that's possible! You're the devil incarnate!"

He lifts the brim of the hat and smiles at me as if I am the sexiest woman in the room, not one hellbent on killing him.

Unfortunately, now is not the time: we're surrounded by so many people. This is hell on a dance floor. As I'm twirled, my vision spins with Lara and Shaun grinning, arms around one another, a cluster of bridesmaids and groomsmen clapping, grandparents, parents, children. Sam leans me backwards as he murmurs in my ear, "Forget everyone. Focus on the me."

"I hate you," I hiss. "How's that for focus?"

"Baby, we aint even started."

He loosens his bowtie and lassoes it around my shoulders, bringing me closer still. Oh good Lord, he has a look in his eyes. I think he's going to kiss me...in front of everyone.

"Don't you dare," I snarl, shutting my eyes.

A cracking noise beside me makes me jump. It's Sam's bowtie. He tosses it at Lara. She yeehahs and hollers as she twirls it around her head.

Crap. "Just how naked are you going to get?" I mutter as he pulls me in close and whirls me around again.

"Honey, try to remember this is not for you. Keep moving those hips, please, and whatever you do, don't drop my hat. I'm going to need it," he growls in my ear.

No! No! No! I want to weep, but I fix my mouth in a rigamortis smile and somehow keep dancing. Very badly.

Thankfully, while I'm doing an awkward jiggyjiggy disastrous disco, all eyes are on Sam. He leaps, does a full graceful whirl around the pole and then a long slide to the other side of the dance floor. *Wow.* Even I have to admit, that was actually pretty incredible. Not facing me, dancing with the audience, he kicks off shoes and socks. I have to give him more credit: not many men could manage to make taking socks off look sexy, but somehow he nails it.

Then he turns to face me, eyes burning, smile one hundred percent pure Kiwi evil.

No. Oh please no. Sam slowly starts popping the buttons on his shirt; I think I might explode with embarrassment. Snaking his hips, he gyrates in my direction never taking his eyes off mine. A slice of torso appears. A shoulder. His bare chest. Then the shirt is off and thrown in my face.

By the time I disentangle myself this time, Sam is literally climbing the pole above my head with only his hands, all in rhythm of the music, and if that's not spectacular enough, he's rotating around it at the same time. It's death defying. *Holy holy ... He's astounding.* He hooks a knee around the very top, and for a heart-stopping moment he free falls — there's a communal gasp from the audience — but his outstretched hands save him. Gripping onto the pole, he arcs smoothly around it at an impossible angle upside down. He lands on his feet and dances toward me, face looking ominously ... serious.

I want to be throw up. At least, I'm salivating which is a pretty good indication. He's about the most perfect male specimen I've ever laid eyes on, but that only makes it so much worse. His pants are shucked off — Was there velcro involved? — and thrown elsewhere into the crowd. Sam wearing just some tight black boxer shorts twirls me around and leans me backwards again. There's only his hat between me and his bare torso.

"I'm not sure I've ever seen anyone look so terrified. Going to loosen up any time soon?" he asks.

"And d-do what? Don't drop me!" I squeak.

"I was told you could dance." He twirls me around.

"I c-can't pole dance and I'm certainly not stripping. It's challenge enough just keeping hold of this hat." I want to run screaming from the room, but until the music ends I'm stuck here, struggling even to breathe.

"Just lie at the bottom of the pole and try to look sexy. If that's not too much to ask."

Dancing, always dancing, he trips me into his arms again and lies me gently down, leaving me in a limp exhausted pile at the pole base.

Launching himself upside down above me, legs stretched in a wide 'v' he climbs the pole above me using only the strength of his arms. His biceps are a sight to behold. He spins in the air as gracefully as a gymnast. It's mesmerizing. Spellbinding. Gravity-defying. And absolutely terrifying. The muscles on the man strain and bulge and defy my understanding of anatomy. It's too damn hot on this dance floor for anyone mortal.

At the top of the pole he looks down and locks eyes with me. "Throw me the hat," he calls.

"Now?"

"Yes, now!" He grins.

I toss it upwards. It's a terrible throw. I gasp, heart stopping altogether, as he plummets toward me down the pole, catches the hat, and slides into a one-handed press-up over the top of me our faces just millimeters apart.

Oh my God. I stop breathing. I may have had a heart attack.

Sam is panting, but he smiles. And puts the hat on his head. The music ends. He completes his press-up lowering this lips to mine. There is a riot of applause.

I guess he has done this routine a thousand times before. "I can't even...!" I hiss into his face.

"Couldn't have done it without you," says Sam, as he leaps up and pulls me to my feet. "You were awesome." Or did he say *awful*? I am dizzy. Seeing stars and flashing lights.

"Though I have to say, sweetheart," he says out of the corner of his mouth, "you can't throw for shit." He bows to his adoring audience.

A crush of people rush toward us, congratulating Sam because, let's face it, I don't think I'd even constitute window dressing. I need air. Clean, fresh air, unpolluted-by-Sam air.

7

I fight my way through the crowd making a beeline for the bar. "I'll have a double Jack Daniels straight up, please," I say.

"Yaaas! Didn't you love the dance? Wasn't Sam awesome?" gasps Lara coming up beside me.

Face focused on the ceiling, blinking back my tears of humiliation away so Lara doesn't see them, I turn to smile at her. "He's incredible," I agree. I don't know why I feel like crying. It must be the adrenaline. I need to get over myself.

"What's the matter?" asks Lara. We might not have seen each other for a few years, but she still reads me better than almost anyone.

"Nothing. He was astounding. Very ah ... talented."

"Noelle." She links her arm through mine and rests her head on my shoulder. "What's up?"

"Okay. He's an amazing dancer, but we sort of got off on the wrong foot already and I could have done without that dance. I think he was deliberately trying to humiliate me."

"What? How? The pair of you looked..."

"Let's be honest, I looked like a lame donkey."

She laughs. "Not true. You were good. Admittedly, it was hard for anyone to take their eyes of Sam, but ... I'm sorry. This is my fault. I warned Shaun you might not be happy being center of attention. Now I've ruined everything."

I put an arm around her and take a swig of my drink. "Don't be silly. You haven't ruined anything. It's been a wonderful day."

She bites her lip. "Really?"

I nod. "Really."

"We were really hoping the two of you would hit it off. Forget about Cole. Don't you think Sam's jacked?"

I laugh. "He's a jackass." And hearing how bitter it sounds, I have another slug of my drink. "Uh, not going to happen. Please don't try to set me up with anyone. Especially not Sam. I'm not interested. I need a break from guys altogether."

"Okay, I won't. I promise. But, give him a chance. He's a nice guy. I reckon you'll be good friends once you get to know him better."

"I know him better than you think." I pause and stare into my drink wondering whether or not to confess. "I sat next to him on the flight over."

Lara's eyes widen. She gawps. "What? He never breathed a word. Really?"

"Yes, really. I guess he doesn't tell you and Shaun everything ... like the fact he was rude to me to the point of being obnoxious. The man is a toad."

She frowns and pouts simultaneously. She looks uncomfortable. "Oh."

For a moment we lock eyes and I feel bad again.

"I'm sorry. I'll tell Shaun to cancel everything," she says.

"Like what?"

"Uh, I may have asked Sam to keep an eye on you while we're on honeymoon. He's our closest neighbor and I sort of asked him to show you around... and I may have already booked a couple of activities..." She bites her lip and starts to look tearful. "Never mind. I wouldn't want to force you to—"

I close my eyes and count to three. "Did Sam agree to it?"

She nods. "Mmm-hmm. I think he helped Shaun come up with some of the ideas. If the pair of you don't get on, I've no idea why."

I do. It's twofold. One, to humiliate me some more, and two, he's trying to keep his friends happy. I'm not so kind. "Look, that's really thoughtful of you, but I was kind of counting on having some down time."

"Okay. Though it seems ... like a crying shame...coming all this way for some down time. When are you next going to be in New Zealand? Why come all this way and not even see the place? That's not like you."

She has a point.

I inhale wearily. "What sort of activities did you have in mind? It'd better not involve a pole."

Lara smiles beneath her eyelashes. "No. I promise." She lowers her voice "When I mentioned to Shaun that you wanted to show Cole how adventurous you could be, you know after that *vanilla* comment, Shaun suggested a jet boat ride, a bungee jump, and, or canyoning."

I grip hold of the bar. "You did not tell Shaun about the vanilla comment."

Lara doesn't reply. Crap.

"That's super generous of you both, Lara, but I'm not really—"

"What did you say in your speech? If you don't give things a go and take a few risks, Nol, you'll never find out how much you might enjoy yourself. You said you wanted to prove Cole wrong. This is your chance to make him jealous. You said you wanted to spice up your life. Besides, I don't think we'll be able to get our money back now."

Oh. I knock back the rest of my drink. "I can reimburse you."

"There's no need. If you really don't want to go ... Although, I think this'd be good for you. And you'll be safe as houses with Sam. Like you said, he's not interested in you in that way." She pulls a face. "Please! For me! I want you to love your time here." Her doe eyes look up at me.

This is one sure way of making sure I never come back.

"Okay," I say, sighing. "If you really think so."

"Awesome. I'll go and give Shaun the good news." She scurries off and I order another drink.

In the corner, I spot Sam chatting to some blonde lady. She's batting her eyelashes and gazing up at him adoringly; I'm ready to dump his ass in deep water.

"Excuse me, excuse us," I say, interjecting myself between them so the lady is looking at the back of my head and I am glaring right at Sam. "So sorry to interrupt this *tête-à-tête,* but we need to talk. Right now. About our plans for the next few days."

Sam frowns.

"I think you owe me that at least, don't you?" I hiss.

"Do I?"

"After our little twirl around the dance floor, yes, I believe you do. I need to talk to you about the itinerary you've come up with with Shaun."

"It had nothing to do with—"

I turn away and stalk outside and trust he's following. I stomp to the end of the jetty, so I can shout without an audience.

"What the hell were you thinking? Canyoning? Bungee jumping? Do I look like someone who'd get off on bungee jumping? Is this some sort of vendetta against me just because—"

"I didn't know you were you when I suggested those things to Shaun. I only found out you were you when I saw you at the wedding. We booked some common tourist activities in this area."

"Bull! Like you didn't know it'd be humiliating for me to be paired with you in a pole-dance freak show."

He folds his arms. "Freak show?"

I try not to look at his biceps. "You're totally transparent!"

His eyes narrow. "After listening to your speech earlier and from the little I know of you from the plane, I'd have thought this would be right up your alley ... Aren't you desperate to impress your ex?" His smile doesn't reach his eyes, and I can't help wondering how much he knows. "Believe me, the itinerary is tame compared to what we could be doing."

The way he says it has me snarling. I poke him in the chest. "If you think for one second, I'm going to waste any more time being humiliated by you, doing all these ridiculous schoolboy stunts, you can think again."

"Fine. Don't you worry about Lara and Shaun being upset because they've wasted their money. They even asked me to send photos."

"You'd better find yourself a stunt double then because I'm not doing any of it."

"I'm not sure I could find a double for the likes of you," he says, and not in a nice way. "*Life should not be boring. It should be an adventure. We could all do with some of that,*" he starts mimicking my speech.

With Sam mocking me, it's a challenge to get enough oxygen into my lungs, and the whole mad, crazy wedding Down Under feels like it's gotten totally out of hand. My head buzzes. My fingertips fizz. I stamp my foot. "Are you always such an asshole?"

"Are you always vanilla-*ahhhh!*"

Without thinking, I have shoved him in the chest.

Sam's eyes widen in alarm, his arms wheel and instinctively he grabs hold of the nearest thing to him — me.

Time slows.

Horrified, I stare at his incredibly handsome, incredibly shocked face before the cold water envelops us like an iron fist.

It's pitch black. Instinctively, I thrash my arms and legs, but I'm not sure which way is up or down and my limbs are snagged by swirling fabric. I fight and expect to break the surface any seconds, but instead the breath is squeezed from my lungs and I open my mouth to gulp air, but swallow water. Flailing like a fish on dry land, I realize I'm sinking, I'm going to die at my best friend's wedding. Could anything be worse?

Someone grabs my arm and yanks. I'm hauled to the surface.

Choking, coughing and spluttering, I gasp for air, but my lungs are water-logged. I'm vaguely aware of being pulled along in someone's wake, a firm hand grasping under my chin as the world begins to dim.

"You're okay. You're going to be just fine," says a heavenly voice in my ear.

8

I don't know why I was so worried about the plane crashing, or my pole performance: my near death experience in Lake Wakatipu brings everything into sharp relief. Someone thumps my back, and I lie on my side hacking up water. I've been dragged from the lake and dumped on the grass lawn. I can't stop shivering, but rolling onto my back I'm grateful, so bloody grateful, to be alive. I catch my breath, staring at the stars overhead, thinking how beautiful the night sky is, and how lucky I am.

Lying next to me, Sam scoops me up against his chest and holds me close. There's something deeply reassuring about the damp warmth of his chest, the heavy rise and fall of his chest and the drum beat of his heart. We don't talk. Maybe tomorrow I'll feel differently, but right now, I'm grateful he's here and I'm not alone. I deserve worse. The worst. I can't believe I pushed him into the water ruining his evening more than mine.

"It was an accident," I hear Sam say some time later. "My foot slipped and I dragged her in with me."

No-one questions his version of events.

I'm bundled into towels and put in a car.

Gladys offers to find Lara. "P-p-please d-don't!" I'm ashamed enough already. And I'm not cold, but a voice in my head tells me I'm in shock because I keep repeating, "I'm perfectly fine," through chattering teeth.

There are offers of help from some of the other guests, but I'm surprised when Sam gets into the driving seat.

"I told you, I'm fine," I say for the hundredth time before curling up in the back seat, too weak with remorse to complain any more.

Either I'm incoherent or Sam chooses to ignore me. The pair of us are dripping all over the car upholstery. His car. I half expect him to read me the riot act so I close my eyes, Shame and guilt sober me up. I've not exactly been the perfect maid-of-honor I set out to be. A moan escapes me.

"You alright? You're not going to be sick are you?" murmurs Sam.

"No. You worrying about me ruining your car interior?"

His chest rumbles with soft laughter. "Bit late for that. We're almost back. I think you'd better sleep at mine tonight, so I can keep an eye on you."

"There's no need. Seriously, I'm okay."

"You've had a nasty shock."

"I'll sleep it off."

The car pulls up outside Lara and Shaun's house. We both get out.

"Stay there. I don't need your help...any help. Thank you for the lift."

There isn't the slightest breeze, but I start shivering again. Best to keep moving even though my legs feel like jelly.

I can sense Sam watching me as I head toward the house. "Night Noelle."

I raise a hand and don't look back. I stand in front of the door and start to laugh. A little hysterically.

"Need a hand?" says Sam.

I rest my head on the door. "My evening bag. I left it ... and my phone ... and the house keys at the wedding!" I'm glad it's dark. The last thing I need is Sam's reproving stare, or him seeing the tears which have sprung to my eyes again. As if I wasn't waterlogged enough already.

"Like I said, you could always ... There's a set of spare keys at my house. I'll go and get them."

I stand halfway up the drive looking at his dark silhouette disappear. After a little bit of staggering up the steps to the deck, I sit down to wait. The night is balmy. The moonlight outlines mountain and lake and the sky is strewn with stars. It's as if my accident has peeled a veil from my eyes. My senses are heightened to the cicadas and the scent of rosemary. I close my eyes.

Next thing I know, I'm being scooped up and carried. I could say something, grumble a protest, but apart from feeling wrung out, I like being carried by Sam.

"You don't need ... but thank you," I mumble.

He carries me inside.

"Put me down." For a moment he seems to hesitate. "Sam, put me down."

We stand looking at each other warily.

"I'm sorry," I say. "I shouldn't have pushed you. You didn't deserve—"

"No, I'm sorry. I was the one pushing you. Verbally. You didn't deserve that." His voice is tender. "You sure you're going to be okay?"

"One hundred percent."

He steps forward and kisses my forehead.

When I wake up next, I am very much alone with my hangover. Rafts of sunlight through the shutters splinter my skull and although I managed to get myself to bed, I've not had the best night's sleep. Tragically, I seem to have spent most of it reliving the previous evening. I assess the damage. How awful was my pole-dancing humiliation? Was there photographic evidence? For that matter, did anyone take photos of me being dragged from the lake looking like a bedraggled poodle? Was there any chance anyone I knew back in the States would ever find out? Quite possibly. My stomach roiled. What would it be like when I next saw Sam? Would be be angry? Resentful? Amused?

Lately, I seem to have no problem making a prize fool of myself, mostly within his vicinity. Remembering how I'd pushed myself between him and that eager-looking blonde, I groan. I more or less derailed his entire evening. Unless he went back.

Downstairs on the kitchen counter I find a note.

Winery have your bags. Will bring them over later this morning. Sam

No trace of sarcasm. No romantic flourishes. No nonsense.

After showering, I stand nursing a coffee staring at the reflections in the lake. My mind skitters back to the wedding. What sort of couple has pole-dancing featured at their wedding? A whole original one. Lara and Shaun know exactly what they want and aren't afraid to flaunt it. I can imagine my mother's scathing expression when I tell her. If I tell her. I'm feeling both emotional bruised, but also kind of protective this morning. Imagine how she'd flip her lid if I told her about Sam, the pole-dancing club owner stuntman. She'd have a hernia. But inexplicably, the idea of Sam, even a belligerent Sam, feels a little like standing in a warm pool of sunlight.

He literally saved my ass last night ... and saw me safely back here ... and carried me inside ... and has now gone to hunt down my handbag. I thought I hated him, but this morning the world seems brighter, the air sharper, my mood lighter. I'm not sure which should make me cringe more, imagining my parents' reaction to everything that happened yesterday, or imagining what Sam must think of me — not only a princess, but a total screwball — and I'd like to help him change his mind.

Staring at the epic scenery, it dawns on me that no matter how much people like my parents might criticize her, Lara has done much more with her life than I ever have or will. She's not gagged and bound by stupid, hidden codes of behavior and etiquette. She's not afraid to be herself. Her love for Shaun is something worth celebrating.

Oh my God, I think I might be jealous of her. How on Earth did that happen? Was there an earthquake last night which shifted the ground.

I'm disgusted by the person I was yesterday, judging Lara on just about everything, looking down my nose like I have anything better to offer the world. It's me who has the issues. It's me who is small-minded and boring. Lara is literally pole-dancing her way through life. She looks fantastic and she's married to the man of her dreams. I'm uptight and too afraid to do anything which might cause a ripple let alone a stir.

I rinse my coffee mug. If an opportunity presents itself, I tell myself, I'm going to be open-minded and see where it leads me. From today, from this very moment, I'll start trying to be more adventurous and, dare I say it, less vanilla.

Just then, I hear the crunch of tires on gravel and a motorbike pulls up the drive.

Moments later, Sam, clad in leathers with a helmet under his arm, walks through the front door.

My stomach somersaults and I look away. "Ever heard of knocking?" I say before I can help myself. I bite my lip. Not really the open-minded adventurous spirit I was just telling myself I wanted.

"Morning, Sunshine. Force of habit. Don't usually bother knocking when I come to see Lara and Shaun." He dumps his helmet and my bag on the counter. "Your stuff."

"Thank you."

"Took longer than I was anticipating because I ran into the happily married couple. They send their love. They were just heading off to the airport."

"Lucky them. I mean to be going on honeymoon. On holiday. I would not want to be going on honeymoon. Anyway, coffee?" Good grief, what is wrong with me?

"Sure. Black please. So what are your plans for today? Taking things easy?"

"Actually I thought I might take a hike. I'd like to see more of the area while I'm here. Don't want to waste this opportunity."

Sam, leaning against the kitchen counter, raises his eyebrows. "If you'd like, you could join me. No pressure. I was going to take a walk up to some waterfalls."

"I know Lara and Shaun asked you to look out for me, but you really don't have to."

"I know I don't have to. But it's not a problem."

"You sure you want me tagging along? I might slow you down."

"Might not be a bad thing."

"And you don't much like my company."

He laughs. "Perhaps, it's time to bury the hatchet."

"In my head?"

A bark of laughter escapes him. I can't help grinning in response.

I take my time making his coffee, feeling awkward under his scrutiny. When I hand the mug over, I can feel heat suffusing my cheeks. It's difficult to meet his eyes. "Honestly, I'll be fine by myself. I don't need babysitting."

Sam takes the mug and puts it down on the counter. "Look, I think I'm possibly Shaun's little project as much as you seem to be Lara's. They're very keen for us to spend time together and become friends, aren't they? Shaun thinks you could be good for me. But if I didn't want to do it, I wouldn't."

"I got the impression he didn't approve of me. Lara must have worked really hard to convince Shaun I'm nice."

"Nice? I know you're not nice." A slow smile spreads across his face as he blows on his coffee. He looks at me over the rim and there is such a roguish glint in his eyes that my heart begins to gallop and I have to turn away to hide whatever the heck this is I'm feeling.

"Here's the thing," he says. "You'll be doing me a favor. If we take a hike together and send Lara and Shaun a couple of photos, maybe they'll leave us alone. "Of course, if you'd rather go walking by yourself, that's cool as well," says Sam. "I'm sure they'll totally understand."

And then it'll look like I'm the one being difficult. I take my time deliberating.

"Thanks for the coffee," says Sam. How has he already finished a scalding mug of coffee? He picks up his helmet and heads for the door.

"Um... I don't suppose it's the worst idea I've ever heard, and I could do with a tour guide."

He pauses and looks back at me. "Great, I'll pick you up in an hour," he says and strides outside to his motorbike with a cheery wave. "Don't forget your swimming togs, Princess!" he shouts.

I watch him mount the bike. Those leather-bound thighs do something wicked to my insides.

9

After our unexpected dunking the night before, the last thing I want to consider is going swimming, but there's no way I'm letting Sam keep calling me Princess or thinking I'm scared for that matter. Time to confront my fears head on. It's not as if I don't know how to swim. Last night I was simply taken by surprise. Maybe spending the day with Sam is not such a bad idea even if the thought is giving me butterflies.

"Help yourself to everything while you're housesitting," Lara had said before her wedding, so I do. Putting on my bikini, I rummage in Lara's hiking gear because I have nothing remotely suitable for walking. Her feet are slightly bigger than mine, but I wear two pairs of socks to compensate. By the time Sam knocks on the door I've made a pack lunch for two and I'm good to go.

"Okay. I've never been on a motorbike before," I admit to Sam.

"I'll take it easy. All you have to do is hang on."

For some reason, that notion bothers me, but I clamber on behind him and wrap my arms around his torso.

I try not to dwell on the muscles on the man as we ride to the end of the road and then through a gate and onto an unsealed lane. I'm forced to cling on tighter as Sam navigates uphill on a track which eventually peters out altogether. Sam parks the motorbike under some trees and without any consultation with me, he sets off on foot. I trail in his wake up the track which narrows into a footpath and then little more than a goat track.

He's walking at a blistering pace, probably trying to lose me. Occasionally I have to jog to keep up, but Sam stops every so often to take photos on his phone. I'm thankful when we hit the treeline again because I'm already working up a sweat and it's so much cooler in the shade.

We stop for a drink, and I strip down to my tank. We've only been going for an hour and I already feel like I'm wilting. "Where are we headed?"

"Kind of a special place. A waterfall and swimming hole. Shaun and I used to camp up there as kids. It's off the beaten track and not many people know about it."

"Sounds good." Though maybe not so good as a spa day and massage. "How long have you and Shaun known each other?"

"Since high school. There were a bunch of us who were into parkouring around the school yard."

"Parkouring? That thing where you jump around and look acrobatic in urban spaces, right?"

He gives a slight roll of his eyes.

"Excuse my ignorance. Do enlighten me."

As we continue on our hike, Sam explains parkouring. Apparently, it's about getting from one point to another in the fastest and most efficient way possible without any equipment to make things easier. "It comes from the French term *parcours du combattant* meaning obstacle course."

I can't help correcting his French accent. "I have a French mother," I explain.

He gives me a look. "It's really just about overcoming obstacles, mentally and physically, and some of us have more than others…" His stride lengthens again.

"So how did the leap from parkouring to stunts happen?" I ask, jogging a few steps.

He doesn't slow. "Met a girl in a club who was a pole dancer. She persuaded me to give it a go. It's another great way to keep fit and build body strength. I told Shaun about it."

"And that's how Shaun met Lara, and the rest, as they say, is romantic history!" I rest my hands on my knees. When I look up, he snaps a picture of me gasping for breath. "Seriously? I'm a sweaty mess here. Could we at least send Lara and Shaun a more flattering picture?"

"What're you worried about? You look great." He shows me. Half my hair is glued to my face, my cheeks are pink and I'm shiny with sweat.

"That is awful."

'Well, it's photographic evidence for Lara and Shaun." He keeps walking.

"What you need to show them you're keeping your word and looking after me?" I ask.

He doesn't answer.

I know I look a mess, but I can't help smiling as his exact words come back to me — it may have been a slip of the tongue, but he said I looked great. I bet Cole would be horrified at my current state. Or would he?

As I huff and puff my way up a hill, my mind works overtime. I should be taking more photographs and plastering them on social media. I must not forget my self-marketing campaign. It's a great idea, if I can get the right kind of shots. The sort of images which would catch Cole's attention and make him realize he's overlooked me. And if I'm being totally honest, Sam makes perfect arm candy. Hmmm. That's definitely an idea worth exploring.

Sam has stopped up ahead and watches me approach. He takes a couple more shots on his phone and I flick him the bird. He laughs. "Do you think you're up for another swim?"

"I don't know." My stomach has started whirlpooling at the thought and beyond Sam is the thunder of a waterfall. He's standing on a cliff edge and below is a pool where the water looks crystal clear, a beautiful turquoise. It's picture postcard perfect. Me, Sam, waterfall and blue skies.

"Let me take some photos on my phone this time. I'd like one with the waterfall in the background."

I turn around and, hot damn, Sam's stripped off already. He's in board shorts, and I'm face-to-face with his naked torso. It's like the whole pole-dancing experience all over again, except now we're alone and miles from anyone.

"Sure." He comes and stands beside me.

If my cheeks are burning it's no surprise, but petty-minded as it may be, I focus on how this'll make Cole feel. "Maybe you should put an arm round shoulders so we look a bit more pally. For Lara and Shaun's sake."

My hand trembles as I take the shot. "Could you take it? You're taller."

Sam snaps a couple more pictures. I lean back between both his arms and adopt a blissed out pose.

He hands the phone back. "There's a path down to the right," he says, pointing out a narrow track. "I'll meet you at the bottom."

"Where are you going?"

He hooks his thumb over his shoulder toward the cliff edge.

"You've got to be kidding!"

"It's safe. I've jumped hundreds of times."

I blink and look down. "How high up are we?"

"Only about four or five meters. Nothing to land on except water. And me. If that doesn't give you incentive, I'm not sure what will." He smiles and my stomach does a flip all of its own.

"Well, that's not exactly reassuring—"

Sam takes a flying leap. My heart seems to leap with him. He's so graceful like a diving bird and then he carves through the water below. He surfaces seconds later grinning. "I dare you. Come on. It's fantastic. Jump!"

I peer over and swallow. It's seriously a very long way down.

"If you want we can do the jump together." He starts swimming to the base of the cliff.

I'm not going to jump. Is he nuts? After last night, getting in the water at all feels like a big deal in itself. But Cole's 'vanilla' comment flits through the mind and I can't bare the thought of being so tame and conventional. Before I know it, I'm stripping down to my bikini, my determination to be more 'open-minded' to opportunities and adventure on full volume in my head. "Has Lara ever done this jump before?" I call.

"Oh, sure. Heaps of times."

Of course, she has. But I take my time. I have to walk away from the edge and berate myself for being so weak. So fragile. So lacking in backbone. I glimpse over the edge again and immediately my hands start shaking and my knees turn to jelly.

I gasp as Sam unexpectedly climbs back over the lip of the cliff edge and stands in front of me, water trickling in rivulets down his muscled torso. Hot damn.

"Want to give it a go together?" He looks at me, with earnest encouragement shining from his eyes, and I have to tear my gaze away from him.

I swallow. "I don't know. Maybe. I'm not sure I can." What am I saying? Am I trying to prolong this pretense that I'm not scared, this fleeting feeling that he might think I'm maybe someone worth spending time with. I don't want to be a princess. I want to be brave.

He takes my hand. On legs like quivering reeds, I edge toward the drop, uncomfortably aware of Sam beside me and the water a long long way below.

"I have to be honest, I've never done anything like this before." My voice is mighty squeaky all of a sudden.

"Don't overthink it, remember," says Sam. "You could just step off and it'd be fine. Trust yourself. Trust me."

"Right, trust myself." I remove my hand from his, shake out my arms and flex my shoulders.

"Would you like me to hold your hand?" asks Sam.

"Is that a serious question!" I snap, glaring at him. Oh lord, his eyes are as warm as the sun on my shoulders. "Sorry. I don't do this sort of stuff. It scares the hell out of me."

"You don't have to do it."

"But I want to!" I really want to, even though my eyes are pooling with tears and my legs are trembling. I start muttering a mumbo jumbo of prayers.

"There's no shame taking the path down, Noelle."

"The easy path. I'm sick of taking the easy path. I'm tired of being vanilla. Let's do this."

"If you're not ready, don't force—"

I jump out as far as I can. My stomach lurches upward as I plummet downward. I hit the water like a sack of potatoes and I'm swallowed up by the icy cold. I never touch the bottom. I kick my legs and start to panic. It's like last night all over again. I've been plunged into an icy grave. The cold water clutches my chest, holding me down. Something dark rockets through the water past me in a jet of bubbles scaring me even more. Thrashing my legs and arms madly, I claw my way in the opposite direction, up toward the sunlight. Finally, I break the surface, gasping for air.

Sam surfaces at the same time, and I realize he has one hand under my arm, treading water beside me. "Wow. You took me by surprise. I wasn't ready for that."

I start laughing. I think it's the relief that I'm still alive. "I can't believe I did it. I did it!"

But Sam is swimming away. Disappointment hits me between the eyes like an ice-cream headache. He's no idea what a big deal this is for me. I did it!

And it's at that point I realize my bikini is floating on the surface, hanging on around my neck by a thread.

Hastily, turning around, I try to fix it, but it's not easy treading water.

"Need a hand?" Sam is laughing from the safety of the other side of the waterpool.

"No thanks!" I swim to the shallows and retie my bikini. Then I clamber out onto a large smooth rock and sunbake. I might be embarrassed, but I'm actually proud of myself.

The sun is deliciously warm. The rush of adrenaline slowly

drains away. I observe Sam out of the corner of my eye as he explores the pool. He reminds me of an otter. Dark hair sleek and gleaming, sunshine glistening on his skin as he climbs back up the face of the rock we just dived off, before hurling himself off again. Goddamn lunatic.

"Going to have another go?"

"I'll save it for another day. Thanks all the same." Two close scrapes with death in twenty-four hours is more than sufficient. My heart has only just returned to halfway its normal pace and I'm enjoying this moment basking in my own bravery.

By the time Sam is done mucking about, I have more or less dried off.

"We should probably head back," he says, lithely climbing from the water to sit on the rock beside me. "Besides I'm ravenous."

Our eyes meet and he just stares. He's caught the sun, his cheeks suffused with a slightly pink glow. For a crazy second, I think he might kiss me again, but then he's leaping to his feet, clambering up the rocks and over the lip at the top again. That man is half-monkey, I swear.

Now I'm comfortable, I'm reluctant to move.

"Come on sunshine!" shouts a voice from above. "Unless you want to spend the night camping under the stars with me, we'd better get going."

Me and Sam camping under the stars? I don't think so. I'd be in all sorts of trouble.

With a groan, I get to my feet.

10

By the time Sam pulls up outside Lara and Shaun's kitchen window, the sun is setting.

"Hold on. Do you mind if I take one more photo?" I ask.

"Do you think Lara and Shaun need reassuring that I've returned you home unmolested?"

I hesitate. "To be honest, it's not for their benefit. I wouldn't mind Cole realizing what he's missing."

Sam takes my phone out of my hand and snaps a photo of us together on his motorbike. "You know, I think we could both help each other out with something," he says, handing me back my phone.

"What do you mean?"

"Why don't you let me cook dinner for you tonight and I'll explain?"

"I should be the one cooking for you to thank you for looking after me today."

"Okay, so what's on offer?"

"Ah. Cheese and crackers?"

"You come to me. Sounds like a much better plan."

Okay, this sounds like a business arrangement. And I'm more

than a little tempted. Plus my stomach chooses that moment to rumble ominously. Double plus, I don't want to spend the evening home alone and it would be freakin' fabulous to have someone cook a proper meal for me.

"What's your address? I'll order a cab."

"Those are as rare as hen's teeth here, besides, it's only a short walk." He points to the next house in the valley. "That's me over there."

"Oh. Great. Well so long as I can help cook. I'm not the sort of *princess* who expects to be waited on hand and foot you know."

Sam's answering grin releases bubbles in my stomach.

Admittedly my cooking ability amounts to ordering takeaway and passing it off as my own cuisine, but I will watch and learn. This is an easy opportunity to grab. Triple plus, it's not like I need any more reasons, but the shot of us together on his bike looks awesome and perhaps he's got some ideas for more photo opportunities to tempt Cole with.

The red light of Sam's motorbike disappears down the drive and up the one next to ours. I can't help watching him all the way home. I'm still standing there watching when he dismounts. He takes off his helmet and raises a hand.

I wave and practically skip into the house. I've said yes to going hiking, yes to throwing myself off a cliff into deep water, and now yes to dinner with Sam. Whatever next?

I study the pictures of the two of us more closely. Some are slightly out of focus. I think my hand may have been shaking. I reduce the color tones so my face looks less pink. There's no denying Sam looks hot. *Don't overthink it,* I tell myself and post the captioned waterfall photo to Instagram.

Christmas Eve is hot! Taking the plunge at one of New Zealand's secret waterholes to try to cool off...

#HotDownUnder #lookwhaturmissing

Then the one of us on the motorbike.

How to see New Zealand!
   #Whataride #girlrider #lifesaride

♡♡♡

"There must be a way to do this without crying," says Sam, tears streaming down his face as he chops an onion. "Want to take over?"

"Not a chance, I'm on salad duty." I grin. "Besides watching you cry makes me feel the day has not been entirely wasted somehow." I grab my phone and snap a picture of him in an apron with tears rolling down his cheeks.

"You're evil," he says.

"I'm pragmatic." I'm already thinking up more hashtags to annoy Cole with. *#Mantears #don'tcryforme* ... "It'll ruin my mascara and people will think you're dating Kung Fu Panda."

The look he shoots me. Oh shit.

"Not *dating*. Having *dinner* with. And there's not much Kung Fu about me ..." I splutter some and wander over to the open doors onto the patio.

The barbecue is already heating up and my mouth is watering. "So, you said there was something you wanted to discuss. Shall I set the table out here?" I think I need to go outside to cool down. Talk about hot in the kitchen.

"Can do. Cutlery is in the drawer," he says.

His kitchen is rather spartan, probably because he doesn't spend that much time here. At the other end of the room is the sitting area with two enormous old leather sofas. There's a Christmas tree in the corner, but it's not got much in the way of decorations on it. He's not exactly gone to town with the whole festive vibe in the house, but I guess he hasn't got kids to keep happy.

Back turned to me, Sam starts making burgers. I snap another shot.

#Hotinthekitchen #cookingonhot #eatyourheartout

I write a quick post and send it out into the ether.

A post from Cole catches my eye.

"That son of a bitch!" I mutter.

"Excuse me?"

"Sorry, not you. That's *my* desk!" I snarl at the phone.

Cole has posted a recent picture as well. It looks like it could be from a couple of days ago at our work's Christmas cocktail party. He's sitting on my desk with his arm around Vanessa Belmonte from HR. The caption reads,

Wherever you are in the world, wishing you a very merry Christmas. Still hard at work...

Which is when I notice his hand on Vanessa's leg. "Son of a bitch," I say again. He's goading me deliberately. I suppose at least it means he's paying attention to my posts.

"If it's not me, which son of bitch are you referring to?"

"What?...Oh, Cole."

His eyebrows rise. "So, correct me if I'm wrong, but it sounds like you haven't got over this guy at all."

"I have," I say. "I'm just pissed about how he's dealt with everything. It's a long story. He needs to realize I'm not just some fluff..." I stop myself before I start off on a full rant.

"So, my idea. How about spending Christmas Day with me and my family tomorrow."

I'm glaring at my phone. I know he's said something, but my focus is elsewhere. "Mmmhmm...sure..."

"My sisters and their respective other halves and kids. They won't object if you want to take photos. It'll be Christmas Kiwi-style. We'll also be keeping Lara and Shaun happy that we're hanging out and ..."

I look up. "What?"

"And we could stage some photos to make Cole realize what a dick he is."

I can't help smiling at that.

"It's a date then. Well, not a date. Christmas day with my family."

Excuse me, what? What have I just committed to?

"What did you have in mind?"

"Let me get you a drink and we can discuss it some more. I haven't even offered you one yet, and I don't think you're going to want to do this sober."

Oh God, now I'm worried. "Do what sober?"

"Do you like cocktails? Owning a bar, cocktails are my speciality. What's your poison? Rum Eggnog? Christmas Mimosa? Or we could create our very own Christmas Eve special—Maybe we'll call it a Screw You."

I burst out laughing. "Definitely a Screw You. Make it a double on the rocks."

Sam grins back at me. My heart skips a beat. "Why don't you put on some music?" he suggests.

As Sam multitasks between making dinner and making cocktails, I try to forget about Cole and relax. It's a beautiful evening. Sam is in his element: pouring, shaking, stirring, checking the oven, flashing me a smile as he flips the cocktail shaker. The ultimate multitasking millennial man. He's a pleasure to watch.

I sit on a barstool and snap another photo. Oh yes, Cole, eat your heart out. You are going to regret treating me so badly. He'll be begging me to take the promotion and jump back into bed with him by the time I've finished. I can feel the smug smile that has settled on my lips.

The cocktails are delicious and look so pretty. Sam takes pictures of me sipping, staring into the lens of my phone.

Cocktails on Christmas Eve. This one is a Screw You. #Screwyou #cocktailporn #drunkonlife #forgetvanilla

I show Sam the photos. "What's with the vanilla reference about?"

"Nothing!" I squeak.

"Nothing? You almost match the color of your drink." Which is an alarming shade of scarlet.

"Cole may have said something about me ... um ... being a bit ... that smells so good!" I say joining him beside the barbecue. "Anything I can do to help?"

"Nothing. Just chill."

I can't meet his eyes. The tone of his voice has softened and I don't want to see any pity in his eyes. I keep drinking while he barbecues. There is definitely something about a man in an apron. I tear my eyes away from his butt.

"Is there anything you can't do? This is amazing! Don't you miss living here?" He must think I'm such a loser. I wish I could shut up. I know I'm being over-the-top faux happy, chattering away as I take photo after photo of him and the delicious-looking food.

"Hold on. Come here," says Sam. He takes my phone from me and reels me in toward him. Then he wraps his arms around me and interweaves our left hands together. "Smile for Cole, the son of a bitch."

As soon as the photo is taken, Sam releases me but I'm tingling as if he's rubbed my skin with hot spices. The feel of his hard chest pressed against my back. Our interlocked fingers. My brain is reeling.

The photo is great. Unsurprisingly, I look wide-eyed and startled, but I had no idea Sam was ignoring the camera and staring down at me hungrily. Wow. He's good at this posing for camera stuff. The fabulous barbecue is not the only thing sizzling.

I swallow. "What shall I write underneath?" I say. My hands are trembling.

He takes the phone off me again and taps in the words,

Sam is working up quite the appetite. #Hungryformore

"Oh. Yes, thanks. I guess that'll do." I post the image.

Over dinner, sitting under a canopy of stars, prompted by Sam, I explain why I'm not a fan of Christmas. I do my best not to whinge about never having a proper birthday party, and my parents and siblings usually forgetting it's my birthday entirely because they are busy people, but it's a challenge to keep my voice sounding unconcerned. The last thing I want is for him to think I'm not only a spoilt little princess, but some sort of egotistical maniac to boot. It's a bit of shock, sitting there, realizing I desperately want Sam to like me. His opinion suddenly matters. I do my best not to sound like an entitled brat, but Sam makes me unaccountably talkative and nervous. I spill too much and press him to tell me about his childhood and family. The contrast is stark.

He recounts a couple of anecdotes about his siblings and then asks about mine again.

I clam up. "Nothing much to tell."

"Right," says Sam.

Our upbringings couldn't be more different. Sam and his siblings have been brought up by his grandmother and he's clearly been surrounded by love. He may not have had material riches, but he's had what matters most - a caring family. I'm suddenly terrified to meet his siblings. What if they hate me? I won't know how to behave. We don't really 'do family' in our household.

"Do you think it's a such a great idea me intruding on your Christmas Day? Maybe I should let you enjoy your family while you're here. They might not appreciate—"

"My sisters would like nothing more than to think I've found a... beautiful partner. You'd be doing me a favor by joining us. Otherwise, they're going to spend the entire day grilling me and then working out who they can fix me up with before I leave."

"Could be worse."

"Could be a damn sight better." He grins lopsidedly at me. "You have no idea. My family are...wonderful, but also...exhausting. If I already have a woman, they'll be less inclined to interfere."

"Oh. I suppose..." I bite my lip, fumbling over my words, telling myself I'm misinterpreting what he's said, like the fool I am. I'm not his woman. We're going to be faking it. However, judging from the way I'm currently feeling like I'm the proverbial cat on a hot tin roof, it could be a total disaster. "I'm n-not...About your family...they sound lovely, but perhaps we should rethink."

He studies me. "Rethink because?"

Oh God, now I can see from his expression he thinks I don't want to spend time with his family because they're not good enough for a snob like me. "What if they think I'm an opinionated, loud American pain-in-the-ass."

"They'd be about right, but they'd still be happy to meet you." He smiles again and the relief that rushes through my veins is palpable. "And you've nothing to worry about. They won't think that. They'll love you. They'll love you even more if they think I'm smitten." He clears his throat. "If you're happy to play along that is..."

"That wouldn't involve... What exactly do you mean play along?"

He scratches the side of his jaw and for the first time looks slightly uncomfortable. "If you could maybe forget Cole for the day..."

I sit up. "Not a problem," I say.

"Oh. Well then, if you pretend to be interested in me and I pretend to be interested in you, it'll act like a smokescreen. Like I said, whenever I'm back here, my sisters are forever lining me up with friends of theirs as potential girlfriends and I'm so over it. If they think I'm already spoken for, they might ease off a little." He takes a slug of his beer. "We could pretend to be dating. You can take as many photos as you want for Cole, and I promise to be your adoring new man. No-one need be any the wiser. It can be our little secret." He looks me in the eyes. "No harm done. Boom."

Boom goes my heart. Boom. Boom. Boom. I don't need to pretend. I like Sam. Too much. Somehow, even though my mouth is dry, I find my voice. "A mutually convenient business arrangement." I finish my cocktail.

"Exactly."

I chew my lip. Oh God, I'm not very good at hiding my feelings. This could be messy. "We'd have to lay ground rules."

"I wouldn't expect anything else. Can I get you another drink?"

"No thank you," I say primly. "I think I've had enough. So let's be specific..."

He doesn't say anything, so I have to take the initiative. I don't want to get in over my head. "I don't mind a bit of hugging and hand holding."

"So touching is okay?"

"Within limits!" Wow, I'm immediately blushing to the roots of my hair. I can feel the pores of my scalp lift. "I mean certain body parts are *definitely* off limits."

"What about lips?"

I can't help look at his. Hot holy hell. His mouth is perfectly sculpted and his top lip is upturned at one corner. Mildly amused.

"Maybe ... I'm not sure. You mean kissing. A peck would be fine."

He laughs. "Right. A peck. I'm glad we're being very specific about this beforehand because I could have stepped way out of line." He grins from ear to ear. "I guess it's okay to peck. Like a hen." He begins laughing so hard and I can't help giggling. Tears roll down his cheeks again. "Sorry, I shouldn't make fun of you." He pecks me on the cheek. "Was that acceptable?"

I bat him away and get up to help clear the table. I am feeling horribly *vanilla*. I desperately need to change the subject and get our conversation back onto less shaky ground. "So tell me about your family Christmases. What do you generally do? Will there be games?"

We both take plates and bowls back inside.

Sam leans against the sink, arms folded, watching me beneath hooded sleepy eyes.

"What?" Muscles clench deep inside me.

"Would you like there to be games? Should we be specific about that? Are we talking Monopoly or Twister?"

This is not good. Blood is zinging around my veins, and with him looking at me, it's impossible to think straight. Words spew out of my mouth. "As long as you don't put me in any compromising positions, I'm happy to pretend to be your love interest."

The reflection of the lights flickers in his eyes; my heart gallops in my chest.

"But only for Christmas Day. One day only," I continue in a frantic rush of words. "Don't think I'm going to keep this whole fake-love-crush charade game going on after Christmas."

Sam takes my plate from me and places it in the sink. He turns and takes my face between his palm. "One day at a time. Trust me. I don't want anything more from you than this."

And his kiss is light as a feather, and not nearly enough.

11

If there's one thing I know for sure, Christmas Day couldn't be worse than Lara's wedding day, could it? I bounce out of bed and before I do anything else, I ring home.

"Merry Christmas!" I holler into my cellphone.

"It's not Christmas here yet, darling," says Mom. "And I really haven't time to talk at the moment. Our guests are arriving any minute."

How could I forget my parents' annual Christmas Eve drinks party? Well, more of a social *function* that involves lots of business schmoozing and social climbing, than a genuine party. I check my watch. It must be 5 p.m. in the Hamptons. If I know my mother, it's at least a couple of hours before anyone arrives, but no doubt she'll need every second to make sure she's sufficiently preened and primed.

"This evening would've been so much easier if you had been here to help," says Mom, sounding disgruntled.

"I'm sure it'll be just as successful as ever. I look forward to hearing all about it. I just wanted to wish you all a merry Christmas." Nostalgically, I recall how excited I used to get on Christmas Eve when I was too young even to participate in the annual drinks party.

The glitter and glamor of it all thrilled me beyond measure. When had the sparkle of Christmas officially worn off? It was hard to put a date on it but one too many Christmas mornings being scolded by hungover parents and bickering with my siblings had left a bad taste in my mouth.

I wait in vain for Mom to ask me about the wedding, or to wish me a happy birthday...or a happy anything.

"Talk to you tomorrow then, *chérie*. I really must go." My mother ends the call abruptly, and I look at my cellphone in disbelief. Why am I shocked? I should be used to this treatment by now.

I send Lara and Shaun a text wishing them a happy Christmas and at least I get a more heartening response from them.

> Merry Christmas and happy birthday Noelle, babes! Will call you later but right now we're about to throw ourselves down some rapids. I kid you not. Will call you when we get back on dry land. So glad you and Sam are getting on. We left a little something for you with him. So pleased to hear you're going to be spending Christmas Day with him and his sisters. Say hi and a big happy Christmas from us. Have a great time and let your hair down! xx

That last comment seems slightly barbed considering my hair fiasco at her wedding. Maybe it's me being oversensitive. Let my hair down indeed. At the moment, it's springing in curly mayhem all over the place and I'm nervous as hell about the day ahead, especially playing Sam's 'woman'. A snort of laughter escapes me. *As if!*

I make myself a coffee and go to sit on the deck. Moments later, I get a call from Sam himself. "Morning, sunshine. Happy birthday!" I love that he starts singing happy birthday and not anything Christmassy.

"Enough! You have a terrible voice. Thank you." I'm ridiculously pleased he remembered, and I'm also kind of pleased I've finally found something he's no good at.

"I wondered if you'd like to join me for a birthday brunch before my rellies arrive, so we can go over details." There's an nervous tone to his voice I haven't heard before.

"It's kind of early, isn't it? I haven't showered yet."

"Come as you are. You'll look, um, perfect, whatever."

"You're trying too hard to be nice. Why do I feel suspicious?"

He laughs. "Maybe it's in your nature. Get your backside over here, Princess. I have croissants and birthday gifts."

I smile. "I need a shower. I'll be over soon."

"If you're not here in twenty minutes, I'm going to come and drag you out of the shower myself. And don't think I won't."

"Ha." The thought of him finding me in the shower has me on my feet. "Put the coffee on. I'll be there in ten."

Hair still wet, I ring the doorbell and Sam appears. He sweeps me into a hug, taking me very much by surprise. "Happy birthday! And merry Christmas! Come on in."

Body still tingling from the close contact, I follow him inside, half expecting to find his family there. "Was that just a practice run?" I whisper.

Sam grins. "You could say that." He has everything prepared, the table set: croissants, jam, fresh fruit, yoghurt and orange juice laid out. He hands me a large bouquet of flowers and a birthday card. "From Lara and Shaun." The birthday card includes information about a helicopter ride in a couple of days' time.

"Wow. I can't wait for that."

"They gave me the same, minus the flowers. Sorry, you'll be stuck with me yet again."

I smile. "I think I'll just about bare it." *I don't mind at all.*

He slides a smaller box tied with a green ribbon toward me. "From me."

I frown. "You didn't have to get me anything."

He shrugs.

It's a jade pendant, but more of a creamy amber color than green. It's absolutely stunning.

"It's a *matau*," he explains. "Considered lucky for traveling, and a whole lot more besides."

"It's so beautiful. Thank you. I love it."

"Going to put it on then?"

I take it out of the box. "Of course."

"Here, let me do the honors." He takes it from me.

Goosebumps shiver down my arms as he brushes my hair aside and fastens the catch. "Here's hoping this'll bring you some luck today," he says, standing behind me. "We're both going to need it."

I look up at him and try not to read anything into his intense eyes, or the fact that suddenly my breath seems to be caught in my throat. Yesterday, all I could think about was Cole; today, I feel like I'm hopelessly crushing on Sam, walking a tightrope that no stuntman is ever going to save me from falling off. How am I supposed to pretend I'm with Sam, giving him the impression it's all role-play, when actually I'm now wishing this was for real?

♡♡♡

We meet up with Sam's sisters, Ruby and Karina, and their respective families down at the beach. It's just about walking distance from the house, but Sam drives as he has presents and food to take.

After the initial introductions, the volume rises several decibels as they start telling me stories about Sam. Ruby looks like a more petite version of her brother. Karina is red-haired, long limbed and arrestingly beautiful.

"Sam you never told us Noelle looks just like—" begins Ruby's wife, Lizzie, before Ruby plants a hand on Lizzie's shoulder.

"I love that dress," says Ruby. "Where did you buy it?"

I'm wearing a crocheted number with my bikini underneath. The dress doesn't leave much to the imagination, but I figured, as we were going to the beach. "Uh, thank you. I think it's a Magda Booyah."

"Oh. Afraid I've never heard of her. Lizzie, can you slap some sun cream on Benji?" says Ruby tossing her the sun lotion.

Why do I get the impression she's trying to get Lizzie away from me? Perhaps she's very possessive of her wife? Perhaps she has an ulterior motive. Who do I remind Lizzie of?

"Who do I look like?" I ask, Ruby, but she's distracted by their other child, Bella.

The entourage is quite a force to be reckoned with. There's Ruby and Lizzie (very blonde, very dizzy) and their two children, Benji and Bella. And Sam's other sister, Karina, the eldest sibling, who is married to Dave, a dentist from Otago. Their sons, Jet and Blake, have already run into the water.

I'm not used to this much noise and this much chaos. It's a lot to take in, and Sam's sisters' curious glances make me slightly apprehensive. While gathering up discarded wrapping paper from all the present that have just been unwrapped, I listen to their banter.

"Can we play cricket now?" asks Jet, dripping wet.

"Give us a chance to relax first," says Karina. "Why don't you do some boogie boarding?"

For the next hour, the kids come and go, grabbing extra food before tearing off toward the water and the rest of us sit around. Sam gets grilled by his sisters. They want to know what film he's working on and what life in Hollywood is really like and how he and I hooked up.

He tells them an almost true story about us meeting on the plane on the way over and immediately hitting it off. Our eyes meet and I suppress a smile.

Apparently cricket on the beach and swimming in Lake Wakatipu on Christmas Day is a Devine family tradition. I am obliged to join a team even though I have never played cricket before and I'm clueless about the rules.

"I'll teach you," says Sam, pulling me to my feet.

The way he stares at me is mesmerizing. And even I'm convinced he's attracted to me. Not real, I have to remind myself.

As Christmases and birthdays go, this is one I'm going to remember.

The beach is relatively empty, just a couple of other families further along the shore. The sun is shining. The sky is blue. Sam is ... breathtaking. And he and his siblings all get along so well together.

Once Sam has filled in his sisters on his latest work, rigging stunts for Network II, he asks me to help set up cricket stumps. Away from the others, he pulls me closer. "You sure you're okay with all this?"

I would be fine, except he has one hand on my bare shoulder and the other on the small of my back, and I feel like his eyes can see straight into my soul. "Yup."

"Good. Because I'm about to chase you, and if I catch you, I'm going to tackle you to the ground, princess or not, and I might have to kiss you…I'll give you a head start of ten seconds. One. Two—"

"No wait, what?"

His grin is evil. "Three. Four."

I turn around and sprint. In my head, I'm counting: Five. Six. Seven. *Oh my God, he's going to kiss me.* Eight. Nine. Ten.

I increase my stride, but behind me I can hear Sam's pounding feet. Out of the corner of my eye I see the others laughing and looking in our direction. No doubt this is all Sam's idea of a little role-play. And I'm not going to be able to outrun him. I turn around, hands raised in surrender.

Sam pays no attention. He grabs me and throws me over his shoulder. "I owe you, remember. You pushed me into the lake. Now it's your turn."

Laughing hysterically, I wriggle like hell as he calmly walks with me into the water. "No, wait. I've still got my dress on!"

"You call that a dress. I've seen bigger handkerchiefs."

"You're not seriously going to throw me in the water," I say, unable to stop laughing.

"No, I'm just going to submerge you like this. Sam slowly sinks beneath the water.

I come up laughing and spluttering. "You swine! I wasn't ready for that!"

I try to splash him, but he grabs my wrists, pins them behind my back and gently pulls me up against his chest.

"Easy tiger," he murmurs.

We both still. My heart pounds, and I have to do or say something…

"Maybe now would be a good time to kiss me. I mean give me a peck...if..." What am I saying?

I stand in a daze as Sam's grip on my arms loosens. He cups my face between his hands and kisses me. There is nothing 'peckish' about it whatsoever. It's sweet and warm and overpowering. My arms ravel around his neck, my fingers thread into his wet hair and I arch against him. It's over far too soon.

He literally lifts me away from him, gives me an unfathomable look and steps back. "You are..." he says, and seems to be lost for words.

"Awesome?" I suggest, splashing him again.

"And then some." He grabs my hand and leads me back toward the beach.

I'm left feeling tingling and disoriented. More than a little disappointed, not that I want to put on a big display in front of his family, but you know...One thorough kiss and my heart is already dancing. I don't know whether it's because of him, or because the day has been glorious and I've had a couple of Bucks Fizzes with lunch. Maybe it's because the temperature is hotting up, making me light-headed, or perhaps I'm infected by the humorous banter of his siblings. Or it could just be that kiss and the sight of Sam's glistening torso, so close and yet so out of reach...

To my dismay, he keeps smiling at me, or worse, touching me, and being so considerate... The quieter I become the harder he works to please me. It begins to feel like betrayal because I know it's not real. It's meaningless. I miss the disapproving and disdainful Sam. I'm out of my depth. Make-believe is starting to feel too hard to sustain. This is yet another game and I don't know the rules or how to play.

Things come to a head, literally, when the kids demand we must play cricket before we leave. I'm all too happy to concur and jump to my feet. Anything to put a bit of distance between Sam and me. I'm racing for the stumps, trying to give the impression I'm carefree and game and not at all a princess and, yes, okay, maybe just a little bit competitive, when suddenly something collides with my head and I black out.

When I come round, my ears are ringing.

"She looks just like Sleeping Beauty," says one of the kids.

"She looks like Aunt Kim," says another.

"Oh man, yeah! I thought she looked familiar."

"Will you kids give her some air? Scoot!" says Sam's voice.

I open my eyes. The blurred face hovering above me slowly morphs into Sam's creased forehead and worried eyes, framed by a blue, blue sky above.

"Noelle. Thank God." He kisses me again. "You had me worried."

I can't speak because I have tunnel vision and the only thing I can focus on are Sam's lips and how utterly divine, *Devine divine*, they are. *He* is.

"Say something. Are you okay?"

My head is pounding. I try to sit up and feel dizzy. "What happened?"

"Someone threw the cricket ball at the stumps, and you ran straight into it," says Dave. "Thankfully, your teeth are undamaged."

I groan. Sounds like the kind of dumb idiotic thing I'd do.

"I'm taking you to hospital," says Sam.

"What? Don't be crazy. I don't need to go to hospital. It's just a bump." I make a move to get up, but Sam's hand on my shoulder presses me back down.

"Stay where you are. You have a concussion," says Sam.

"I'm fine!" I do a mental check of my body. I have a headache, but otherwise everything seems to be returning to normal. I don't think I'm going to be running around like some adrenalin-crazed junkie, but I can live with that. The only thing making me dizzy is Sam.

"I don't need to go to the hospital," I mutter, pushing myself up to my elbows. "Get off me!"

Scowling, Sam helps me to my feet. I sway, waiting for the throbbing in my head to recede, and Sam tries to scoop me into his arms.

"Will you put me down?"

"No. You need to rest. I'm taking her to hospital," he shouts over his shoulder.

"You are not taking me to hospital," I say, managing to smile.

"I am."

"You are not. I'm not going to hospital on Christmas Day."

His beautiful mouth compresses into a tight line. Clearly, this is all part of his big act. I let him stagger a hundred yards farther. "Okay, you can put me down now. No-one can see us and I think I can walk."

"I'd rather carry you," says Sam, frowning down at me.

"Is this all part of your evil plan? Was it you who threw that ball?"

Finally he smiles. "I'm not that evil. But you are going to hospital."

The look on his face gives me chills. "Put me down. Put me down, Sam, right now!"

He slows.

"Sam!"

Sam pauses. I wriggle out of his arms, and he sets me on my feet. I tentatively touch my fingers to the side of my head where it's throbbing.

"You should get that seen to."

"I'm fine! For goodness sake! Why are you making such a fuss? The last place I want to be right now is hospital. I'm not going!"

"You must go to hospital. Please." He takes my arm.

I wrench it from his grasp. "What is wrong with you? Get off me. I'm perfectly fine. Perhaps you're the one who should be going to hospital to get your head checked. No, don't you dare touch me again!" I hiss

His shoulders sag and he looks away as if he is in pain. I'm so angry all of a sudden I may have steam coming from my ears and my head feels like it could explode. I'm so sick of men pushing me around and trying to tell me what I must or must not do. If it's not Cole, it's Sam. Who does he think he is? He can't bare to look at me and the feeling is mutual.

Something niggles. Worms its way into my head from nowhere. Prods my conscience with a sharp fork. "Who's Kim?" I ask.

He looks wary. There is pain in his eyes.

"Who's Kim?" I demand. "I look like her, don't I? Who is she?"

"My ex."

I frown. "Your ex?" I feel as if he has thumped me in the stomach. I mean, it's fine for him to have an ex. I know very little about his past love life, but if I look so much like her...that's plain weird, isn't it? "What sort of game are you playing here, Sam? What's going on? I'm very confused."

He's lost for words.

"Exactly how much do I look like her? How long have you been divorced?"

He stares at the sky. He scuffs the sand. I'm shocked by how uncomfortable he looks. He shrugs. "You're similar to look at ... I guess ... but you're nothing like her...We're not divorced —"

"You know what, enough. I don't want to know what she means to you. I've played my part and now I think I need time to myself. This is all sorts of messed up, but I can't think about it right now. Just looking at you is giving me a headache." I know I'm over-reacting but I can't seem to help myself. I feel hideous. I don't just have a headache, I have heartache. I think I might cry. Or possibly throw up. "Please say goodbye to the others," I say stiffly. "Tell them I had a great day and thank you very much."

"Noelle, I—"

I put my hand up. "Shut up. Just wish them a merry Christmas and all that crap. Spin them a line. Whatever line you want to. You seem to have a talent for spinning."

I turn and break into a jog before he sees me crying.

12

Someone knocks on the door. I take a slug of my wine, but don't answer.

"Noelle. It's Ruby. Can we talk?"

Now is the time to go to the door and apologize, but I can't seem to move. Tears fill my eyes. I feel beyond embarrassed, like I'm on the verge of cracking. It's the last thing Sam's sister needs to see. She pounds on the door not going away.

"Noelle, I want to talk to you about Kim."

"Did Sam send you?"

"No, of course not."

I open the door.

"Can I come in," she says. "I've dropped Lizzie and the kids at home, but I wanted to come and have a quick chat. I hope you don't mind."

"No, that's fine. Can I get you a drink?"

"No, thanks, I won't stay long. I just wanted to explain things. You and Sam..."

There is no me and Sam, I want to say.

I trace my finger along a groove between the wooden planks in the kitchen table. "So how similar are Kim and I?"

"You look alike, but your personalities are way different...She was an amazing dancer."

"Thanks. That makes me feel so much better."

"She died after a skiing accident. Sam felt responsible because he didn't take her straight to hospital. She slipped into a coma. Afterwards, he went to America to get over her..."

Oh. God. No wonder he was so insistent. I sigh and put my head in my hands. I feel terrible.

"Anyhow, I gotta go. It's late. I just thought you deserved to know the truth. You going to be okay?"

"Really. I'll be fine whatever Sam may think. I feel fine. But thank you for coming to explain." At least I now know why Sam acted like he did. It makes me sad. I want to weep. He wasn't the only one who totally overreacted. In fact, his concern now seems more than justified.

"For what it's worth, Noelle, he did get over her. You're proof of that."

I'm not proof of anything. I'm a fake.

I listen to the crunch of Ruby's feet on gravel and a car engine start up.

I lie down on the kitchen floor and press my cheek to the cool slates. It doesn't really help. I feel so stupid, so insensitive, so incapable of reacting like a normal sane person. I should have given Sam time to explain. It's like I'm either buttoned up, in a straight-jacket of my own making, or...or a little bit mental and wild.

As far as Christmases go, today has been a rollercoaster. I was on a high, but now I'm plumbing the deepest low. I know I'm not being an adult or rational about this ex-girlfriend thing, but knowing how I should behave and actually doing the right thing is a whole different ball game. I feel like someone keeps moving the goal posts. Changing the rules. I'm damned if I can keep up. All the riches in the world don't protect you from yourself ... and unfathomable heartbreak. I barely know Sam and yet tears spill down my cheeks as if we've been in love forever.

Oh God, now I'm seriously overreacting again. I drag myself up from the floor.

I shower and get dressed in a camisole vest and silk pajama shorts. And then I call my family, because there's nothing like a second dud Christmas call with my mother and father to cheer me up. No-one answers, so I try my sister, Amelie's, cellphone.

"Hey you, traitor, why aren't you here? I am effectively an only child."

"Hey you, happy Christmas."

"And happy birthday to you squirt."

"How was Christmas Eve?" I ask. "Did I miss anything?"

"Only the worst Christmas cocktail party ever. It was hideous." She gives me sufficient details to put a weak smile on my face. "How's your lucky escape going? And more to the point, how was the wedding?"

I fill her in. And I tell her about the whole humiliating Kim doppelgänger episode.

"I made a total fool of myself. Same as I did with Cole."

"No way. Good riddance to Cole. The idiot rang me. Sounded desperate to know when you were coming back."

"Seriously?"

"Seriously. He asked me to ask you to ring him. But please don't."

"I won't. I'm not going back. I think I need a career change." I no longer care what Cole thinks. Cole can wait until the oceans dry.

"Well, that sounds like a no-brainer, hon," says Amelie. "You were miserable at work. I couldn't figure why you were putting yourself through the wringer. I'll tell you what you need to do..."

She knows I hate being told. I sigh. "Pray, do tell."

"Okay. You have to go over to this stuntman's house and perform your own stunt. Or your version of that. You could just offer him your body. Either way, if you care, you need to at least try to sort this out, you moron. Don't hold back. Tell him he could have told you about the ex. Tell him your extreme reaction was because of the bash to your head or the heat or whatever the hell you want. Tell him, you want to finish off Christmas with a bang!" Her laugh is filthy and rather contagious.

Sometimes, even though she can be belligerent and blunt as a truncheon, I love my older sister.

"*Joyeux anniversaire and bon courage,*" says Amelie.

After Amelie and I have put the world to rights, and I've realized that maybe my family isn't *all* bad, I find myself standing at the window and staring across the hillside gazing at Sam's house.

It's late, but there's a light on.

Dare I go over there now? Maybe he's already gone to bed.

And maybe he hasn't.

But like Amelie said, I can't bare how I've left this. There are too many loose strings and things that need to be said. I don't want to sleep on that. I might wake up tomorrow and be my old self again, and I desperately want to at least try to be a bolder, braver version of myself.

Tightening the belt of my thin cotton dressing gown, I walk over to Sam's house and knock on the door.

There's no answer, but the door is unlocked. "Sam? Sam?" I call. "We need to talk." The house is eerily silent, but there is some faint music playing somewhere. Swallowing down my nerves, I step into the kitchen as there is an almighty crash from elsewhere in the house. Toward the back, I think.

I tiptoe through the house in the dark. I'm actually tight with nerves and more than a little frightened. I hope to God he doesn't think I'm a burglar and shoot me. "Sam! Sam! It's Noelle!" I whisper hoarsely.

I find Sam in a room that looks like some sort of home gymnasium though there's the obligatory pole slap bang in the center of the room. Sam is sprawled at its base, one leg wrapped around the pole, an arm wrapped around a bottle of whisky.

I prod him. "Sam? Sam! Are you awake?"

He opens bleary eyes. "I am now." He flops onto his back, throws up an arm and covers his eyes.

"Are you drunk?" I ask. There are fumes coming off him that suggest he should be.

"Not enough," he says, fumbling with the lid.

I prize the bottle from his fingers.

"I'm sincerely sorry about the whole situation earlier, and about Kim. I should've been more understanding," I say.

"Not as sorry as I am..."

"You're sorry for being such a bossy ass or you're sorry I'm nothing like her...I bet she wasn't such a stubborn ... clumsy-mouthed ... terrified of putting a foot wrong...princess."

He lifts an arm and throws me a wan smile. "That is true. You're a total princess." He snatches the whisky bottle back.

I nudge him with my foot. Hard.

"Ow!"

Okay, maybe it was more of a kick.

He takes a slug from the bottle.

"Sorry, I overreacted. I think it was the knock to my head. Sent me a bit haywire." I sit down beside him. "Hey, I have a proposal."

"A proposal. God help me!" Even though his arm is thrown over his eyes, there's the hint of a smile on his perfect lips.

"Don't take this the wrong way. I know it's nearly midnight, but we have about half an hour left of Christmas Day, so what about we make it not the worst Christmas ever? You and me." I peel the whisky bottle from his fingers and take a swig myself, for Dutch courage. It burns my throat and I cough. "Christmas isn't finished with us yet!" I say when I'm done coughing. "We should do something to celebrate."

"What did you have in mind?"

"Well, we should definitely celebrate Lara and Shaun getting married without a hitch ... well, almost without a hitch ... and the fact that neither of us will have to sit next to a complete jerk on our flight back to the States. I mean, the chances of us winding up next to someone worse than each other is less than zero, right?"Without thinking, I take another swig from the bottle and splutter. "Holy smoke, what is this? It's worse than rocket fuel!"

Sam chuckles, then falls silent. Maybe he's thinking. Or sleeping.

Even drunk, he's so good to look at, it makes my heart burn. His t-shirt has ridden up to reveal a taut stomach with sharply defined muscle in a v-shape. My eyes trail downwards...before I tear my gaze away.

I poke him in the ribs. "Come on, Samuel Devine. Wanna play?"

"I'm not a toy, nor a puppy for that matter."

"If only." I look up at the pole I'm leaning against. It looks harmless enough. And sturdy, the metal gleaming in the light. It gives me a crazy idea. "You want to see the worst pole dance ever?"

Sam's mouth twitches. "Do I have any choice?"

I scramble to my feet. "Not really. But I think we need more festive music, don't you? Whatever this stuff is you're listening to, it sounds like a funeral dirge. Come on, it's Christmas and I'm starting to feel merry. Or at least, I'm working on it!"

I flick through his music list and to my surprise find a Christmas playlist. Kind of sentimental for Sam. I look around the room. "It's a bit dark in here. Not very Christmassy at all." I find a light switch by the door and flick it on.

Sam scrunches up his face. "Turn those off. What is this, an interrogation?"

"Don't tempt me."

"You're nothing like her, you know," he says.

"Her being Kim? I know, I'm not really so much of a princess as ... probably your worst nightmare ever."

"The *worst* Noelle," he mutters.

I snap the lights off again and instead turn on the lamp in the corridor outside. Better. It throws a warm amber glow around the room. I study the pole center stage. It gleams, almost winking at me. Probably better not to be able to see what I'm doing. Or not doing, as is more likely the case.

"Okay, you might want to move. If I'm going to do this, you do not want to be in the danger zone."

I grab him by the ankles and attempt to haul him away from the vicinity of the pole. He's immovable, but I do get another 'ow' out of him. "Move your ass, dancing boy. It's my turn to take pole position."

"I can't wait," grumbles Sam, as he rolls onto his hands and knees, and crawls toward the wall. He sits slumped against it, arms folded, eyeing me grumpily under sleepy lids.

"Okay. Get ready to have your bells jingled," I say, and press play.

Dean Martin's voice croons through the darkness.

Singing along to 'Baby, it's Cold Outside' when it is actually sweltering hot is already ridiculous enough without me attempting to swirl around a pole. I swing ... and wipe out on the floor.

Sam chuckles.

I wipe my hands on my shorts and try again. How the heck did Sam, or Lara for that matter, make this look so darn easy? I try to climb higher up the pole, but I'm about as successful as a small elephant and not half as elegant. Out of the corner of my eye, I catch sight of Sam grinning. I remove my dressing gown, fling it in Sam's direction and give him my best twerk.

When I look over my shoulder, I'm pleased to see he's now sitting up, his eyes bolted on me.

"My mother's too busy to worry," I sing, improvising somewhat with the lyrics. "My man just passed out on the floor."

Sam snorts.

"So, really, this is situation is hopeless!" I sing, sashaying my way over to the bottle, "But maybe I'll just swig some more..." I take a swig and splutter. It's so strong!

Sam lumbers to his feet. At least me glugging his whiskey seems to be sobering him up. Fast.

"Say, whatever you think," I sing.

"Oh baby, you're so bad," growls Sam's voice, catching on to the idea and adapting the lyrics.

"Wish I was even worse?" I tease.

He takes the bottle out of my hands and puts it down. "Your eyes are like shining stars," he croons. He doesn't have a bad singing voice, in fact, it has me tingling all over.

"Watch out or I'll break your balls," I sing in response, trying to ignore the fact that now I have his full attention my heart is racing, outpacing the music. I shimmy sexily (as best as I can manage) back toward the pole.

"I don't mind if you to tell me stop," I sing, glancing over my shoulder before attempting another tragic twirl around the pole.

He catches me in his arms before I hit the floor. "Mind if I come closer?"

He's so close. The music continues, but my breath and words are plugged in my throat, and I'm trapped by his hot gaze, conscious of one of my hands against his warm muscled chest, the other trapped behind me on the slippery pole.

Sam brushes my hair out of my eyes. "The worst Noelle, hey?"

"But not the worst Christmas ... I hope."

The song is over. I'm frozen, not even attempting to dance, but holding on to Sam for dear life to stop myself from sliding to the floor in an inelegant heap.

He sets me upright on my feet, but I'm pinned against the pole by his body. "And you call this dancing?" murmurs Sam, leaning closer still, whispering tho words in my ear.

His chest is pressed against mine. Hot tendrils of lust careen down my neck to my core. "Okay, so I dance like a donkey ... Promise it'll be our secret?" It's an effort to talk.

His breath is warm against my cheek. "I could give you lessons in private ... If only you were capable of following instructions."

I gulp. "I hate being told to do anything and clearly, I'm a dancing disaster."

"A prima misdemeanor," he murmurs and pulls my earlobe between his teeth.

I jerk as hot sparks flash through me. He pulls away to inspect his handiwork, a roguish smile playing on his lips. His very luscious lips.

I lick mine without thinking. He blinks.

And I'm suddenly having another deranged idea. Maybe I can blame that on the knock to my head this morning as well, but I want to kiss him again. And more. I want so much more. I want Sam Devine for Christmas.

"Sam, don't take what I'm about to ask the wrong way." I look up.

A broad smile spreads across his face that is like untying a ribbon. "But if I don't ask, I'll never know, right?" I continue recklessly.

"Ask away." His hot eyes light me up like a Christmas tree making it hard to think straight.

"I was wondering, if you'd ever...Um...Have you ever...?"

He takes one of my hands and stretches it high above me. "Oh Princess, this is sounding all too familiar. Mile High Club?" His fingers trace a hot line down my underarm an aside of my ribcage.

"On this pole?" I whimper.

"I wouldn't mind giving it a whirl..." He nips the tender flesh of my underarm between his teeth and I gasp.

"W-what...do you th-think about having a d-different sort of fling? M-more of a one-night stand?"

There's a rumble in his throat. "Are you asking for a friend again?"

"Maybe," I squeak, as he stretches my other arm above my head and pins that to the pole as well.

"Just for Christmas, right?" He trails kisses down my neck and my insides turn to molten lava.

"Or ... w-whenever," I stutter.

"Just a one-night stand?"

"Mm-hmm."

His eyes narrow and his mouth becomes a hard line. "Shit, no!"

"What?" I peer up at my trapped hands. "Then what are you—"

Sam's hand on my lips makes me inhale sharply. As his fingers trail down my chin, and my neck, and my breastbone to my bare midriff, a hot line of fire follows.

"This isn't exactly fair. I'm at a distinct disadvant—" My words are smothered by his lips on my mouth. My heart beats thunderously in my chest. He tastes of whiskey and fire, and my fuse is about to explode. He presses his hips against mine, and it's a relief to feel exactly how much he wants me too.

Hot holy ... hot holy hellll ... and Christmas wishes!

I unravel. I kiss him back as if he's my lost oxygen supply. I'm vaguely aware of him letting go of my hands, my spine still up against the pole as his own large hands tuck beneath my backside, lifting me up until we're eye to eye.

Instinctively, I wrap my legs around his hips and I'm all too aware of his hard pressing hunger as my arms lock around his neck.

Staring into his eyes, I am lost. Pole-axed. Already carried away on a hot tide of lust.

"Nothing wrong with those leg muscles of yours," growls Sam, "but your one-night-stand idea is about as lame as your attempt at pole dancing."

"Oh."

He's stopped. He appears very sober and very serious and very still, and it makes my heart skid. "Then what are we ...?" Does he want me or not? I feel very self-conscious pinned against this pole, my heart fluttering like a butterfly. I'm hyper aware of his grip around my ass. My senses are on high alert, on overdrive, so how could be misreading this situation? Or is this him trying to make a point and teach me a lesson? "Right, well, if you don't want me, why don't you set me down. I can go."

And he does. He puts me down.

Disappointment wells in my chest, hot and uncomfortable.

I try to push past him, but Sam cups my cheeks between his hands and tilts my face, so I'm forced to stare into his eyes again. "Of course, I want you, but a one-night stand is a bloody shitty idea. The worst ever. Because ... a one night with you would never be enough."

"Oh!" I smile, then laugh, my heart palpitating, my knees weak with relief. "For a moment there, I thought you didn't want me. At all."

He groans and kisses me again. Thoroughly. His tongue slides into my mouth igniting flashfires all over my body. Taking a breath, he presses his forehead against mine. "I've wanted you ever since I first laid eyes on you struggling with that bloody oversized handbag of yours."

"I'll have you know, that handbag is Balenciaga."

"Princess, I couldn't give a damn it's Lady bloody Gaga's."

I laugh again but feel awkward under the hot lamp of his gaze. "Where were we?" I say feeling heat rush to my cheeks.

"Are you really sure about this?" he asks.

I nod and bite my lip. "I've never been surer. I want you…I can't think of a better Christmas gift."

He picks me up in his arms. "For you or me?"

"For us both. I'm too heavy. Put me down," I say, although I'm loving every moment.

"Nope. You know what you are? Portable sunshine. I wish I could bottle you," he replies.

"I could be your Christmas spirit. Noelle, the spirit of Christmas! Um, where are you taking me?"

"Upstairs to my bedroom. I want to start unwrapping you."

I laugh again. Suddenly I'm unsure. "You sure having sex in your bedroom isn't too vanilla? Or do you have a pole in there as well?"

Sam bursts out laughing. He laughs so hard that he staggers against the wall. "Oh my God, you really are the worst Noelle!"

In his bedroom, he looks serious. And intent. It's impossible not to admire his biceps as he effortlessly lays me down on his bed. "Sometimes, there is nothing wrong with vanilla." He trails kisses down my neck. "In fact, it's a flavor I love." He trails more kisses along my shoulder. "But what you are, princess, is chili pepper hot … insanely spicy … volcanic … the hottest thing … to derail … my Christmas … ever."

He peels the strap from my shoulder, and I gasp as his tongue rasps over my nipple. "But this … is definitely … not going to be … a one-night anything!" he growls as his mouth and tongue and teeth tease.

Peeling off my camisole top and then my shorts, his mouth travels lower … and who am I to argue?

His lips and tongue and stubbled jaw between my legs trigger sensations that can only be described as a rollercoaster of shock and sublime. I'm strung out taut as a bow, out of my mind, riding an emotion I haven't felt for such a long time — joy! Overwhelming wonderful mind-blowing joy. I cry out, shattering in an iridescent cascade of sparks.

"Now, about those *pole*-dancing lessons..." I say, once I've recovered my breath.

A slow smile spreads across his face as I straddle him.

I unbutton his jeans, taking my time. There's only one pole on my mind. One pole I want to dance around and make my very own. One delicious pole ... and of course, you already know, I'm the very worst Noelle.

THE END

I hope you enjoyed reading The Worst Noelle. If you did it would be really fantastic if you could recommend it to a friend or leave a review.

Ready for your next Anna Foxkirk book? There are other books in the Passport to Love series. Check them out here!

Or if you'd like to hear my latest news please subscribe to my Foxtrot newsletter in which I share not only what I'm up to, but also other author interviews and some exciting giveaways. You can join me here: https://annafoxkirk.substack.com

ALSO BY ANNA FOXKIRK

Passport to Love series

Holly Ever After

The Worst Noelle

Be My Valerie

Alice in Wanderlust

Want to read a snippet of *Holly Ever After*?

Read on …

Chapter One

Holly

I'm standing at the front of class, it's the last period of the school day, one of the boys in the front is frantically wriggling in his chair and waving his hand and my mind goes completely blank. What on earth did I have planned to teach the kids?

"Yes, Charlie?"

"I thought you said we had carol practice this lesson."

"Oh." I knew I had somewhere I had to be. Five minutes ago. "Blow, you're right! We'd better get a move on."

I herd the children out of the classroom trying and failing miserably to look like a calm and collected adult. "Quick, quick, shift your bums … but no running!" Running is not permitted in the hallowed corridors of Burtonbridge School.

Waiting in the Great Hall is Stephanie Dawson, my supervising teacher (and nemesis), and the rest of Year Six. Clearly irritated by our late arrival, she taps her watch. "Come along, Six H, we haven't got all day."

"Sorry! My fault," I gasp, trying to catch my breath after our 'speed walking'. "Right, find a spot. That's it, Year Six, no more than ten of you on each step." I chivvy them up the mahogany staircase of the entrance hall.

There are muffled sniggers. "Year *Sucks*, no more than ten of you—"

"Quiet, Sebastian!" I snap, hearing a little monkey in one of the other class groups making fun of my accent. Being a New Zealander in an English school makes me a constant source of entertainment. I try not to take it personally, even when the teachers have a crack, but it can get a little wearing.

However, right now, we're the ones in the wrong and I don't want to delay things further or dampen anyone's festive spirits. I muster up a cheerful smile, and return to my spot at the bottom of the staircase gazing admiringly at the tiered rows of children. A deep sigh escapes me. Standing beneath the enormous brass chandelier, they look like perfect cherubs and it's impossible not to be swept away by the grandeur of the setting. The wooden banister has been festooned with swathes of green foliage and gold tinsel. Behind them, the afternoon winter sun shines in jeweled shafts through the enormous stained-glass window. The oak-paneled walls, the log fire blazing in the enormous stone hearth, the towering Christmas tree tastefully decorated in red and gold all add to the Dickensian atmosphere of the Great Hall. How incredibly English and traditional the whole scene is. How many years, decades even, has Burtonbridge School celebrated Christmas in this manner? It blows my mind just thinking about it.

A small audience gathers alongside us at the bottom of the stairs, including — I can't help noticing out of the corner of my eye — the principal (known here as the headmaster). Chests puff and the volume of singing increases, including my own. We're nearly done and I'm pelting out the carol along with the kids, feeling immensely proud, when Stephanie Dawson raises her hand bringing everything to a screeching halt.

"What on earth are you singing, Tiffany?"

There is snickering in the ranks. Poor little Tiffany on the bottom step looks terrified. She's one of the youngest kids in my class, a shy girl whose eyes have widened to the size of dinner plates at having been singled out. She glances in my direction, and I smile reassuringly.

"Well, Tiffany?" prompts Stephanie.

"Ah ... Dick the horse ... with...um ... bits of holly, Mrs Dawson?" says Tiffany in her breathy voice.

Stephanie Dawson's shoulders stiffen and the kids fall about sniggering. "*Dick* the horse? Lord preserve us! *Deck the halls*, Tiffany, *with boughs of holly*, boughs like branches, not *bits*! I know you like your ponies, but I can assure you there are no horses in this carol!" She throws me another glare and head down, the headmaster wisely ducks into his office.

Terrific. Once the laughter has been reined in, we continue. *Tis the season to be jolly, fa-la-la-la-la-la-la-la-la.*

If you'd like to keep reading you can grab your copy of Holly Ever After here!

ABOUT THE AUTHOR

Anna Foxkirk is an award-winning author of romcom, fantasy and historical fiction. Her first novella, *Alice in Wanderlust*, was published in November 2020, and in the same year she was voted Favorite Debut Romance Author of 2020 by the Australian Romance Readers Association.

The best way to hear my latest news is through my Foxtrot newsletter in which I share not only what I'm up to, but also other author interviews and some exciting giveaways. Join me here: https://annafoxkirk.substack.com

If you'd like to check out my website, here's that link:
https://www.annafoxkirk.com
And finally, you'll also find me on Instagram:
https://www.instagram.com/annafoxkirk/

A final note...

I hope you enjoyed *The Worst Noelle*. If you did and would like to make my 'happy ever after', please leave a short review on Amazon. It doesn't need to be long, but your feedback is invaluable to me as an author and helps other readers find my fiction. I'd love you to help spread the word!

Before you go, let me wish you all the very best. I hope you read what you love and love what you read!

Warm wishes,
Anna

BONUS SCENE FROM ALICE IN WANDERLUST

"Alice? You still here?" Roger hollers from somewhere in the bowels of the pub.

I pause, a bead of perspiration trickling down the side of my face. Hands immersed in hot soapy suds, I'm in the kitchen out the back of the Jolly Roger Inn scrubbing at pie crust that's superglued itself around the edge of a dish. I listen, puffing at my hair flopping into my eyes, uncomfortably aware of perspiration itching along my hairline and trickling down the sides of my face.

Roger is silent for now, so I resume my scrubbing.

Twister, my twisted twin sister (more fondly known as Tilly by our parents) is proving about as easy to shift as this oven-baked grime. If only I could figure out how to persuade her it's time we moved on. Our year traveling together has ground to a halt. Catching glimpses of my reflection in the window above the sink isn't helping the head of steam I'm building up about our predicament. I want out of Sydney; Tilly seems to have become welded to the place.

I glance again at the clock on the wall. Everyone else has already left the building, except for Roger, the owner of this shithole, and me. I've only been working here for three weeks, but it's been long enough to figure out Roger is only *jolly* when the occasion suits him or when laughing at his own inappropriate jokes. It's amazing that any sane woman would find him remotely attractive, but only last week, Kylie, one of my co-workers confessed, with a snigger, that she'd let Roger have his jolly way with her in a cubicle of the Ladies'. The very idea makes me nauseous. To my mind, Roger's not so much a Jack Sparrow, as Kylie would have us imagine, as Jack Rodent, a scurrying scurvy bilge rat sniffing out his next victim.

If only I'd had the gumption to refuse to work the additional shift this week but lured by holiday rates and the need to pay rent on our apartment (because Tilly never seems to have a cent to her name), I've now worked five consecutive days since Christmas. Roger's take on my situation is that as the new kid on the block I'm not in a position to negotiate, but —Ho, bloody ho!— 'positions are always negotiable'.

I do not want to dwell on the greasy smirk on his face when he said those words, nor the fact he's becoming increasingly matey.

After drying the pans on the draining board, I throw everything back in the appropriate cupboards as fast as I can. Unfortunately, a pan lid clatters to the floor with all the discretion of clashing cymbals.

I freeze.

Whistling and footsteps head in my direction and the hairs on the back of my neck stand to attention as Roger swaggers in.

"Ahoy, my lovely! Still here? Anyone would think you were reluctant to leave me."

"Just finishing off," I say, hurriedly wiping down the worktops, my skin prickling as he leans against the doorframe and studies my every move. How is it, I wonder for the gazillionth time, that Tilly can land a glamorous job singing with a band and serving cocktails in a flashy nightclub, while I'm stuck sweating over dishes and fending off the scourge of Sydney? Oh yes, it probably has something to do with the fact that Tilly is screwing the nightclub owner, Axel.

"Fancy a nightcap, doll?" Roger winks.

I'm never exactly sure if he's calling me *doll* or *darl*, but either way I'd rather walk the plank. "Thanks, but I'm knackered. Not tonight." Not any night.

Drying my hands on my apron, I hang it up. As I shrug into my denim jacket and sling the shoulder strap of my handbag over my head, I'm aware of Roger pulling on his beard. I know I'm nothing to write home about, especially not in my current swampy state, but the way he's eyeing me up you'd think I was drop dead gorgeous.

A thick hairy arm bars my exit from the premises.

"Right. See you tomorrow then," I say.

Roger doesn't budge.

Panic fluttering in my chest, I consider my options. Sadly, I have none of Twister's acerbic wit or tongue-lashing confidence. Despite being her identical twin, she's the sort of siren who can sink a man with a heart-piercing glare or lure him into her arms (and bed) with a provocative whisper. We may be twins, but as far as my understanding of men goes, she was born fifteen minutes and about a hundred light-years ahead of me.

"Come on, Bucko! The night is but young," says Roger.

"I'm exhausted. Roger, excuse me. Please could you let me pass."

Slowly, miraculously, he moves enough to leave a tiny fissure through which I can squeeze, but as I rush towards it, his arm shoots out again. I skid to a halt, my heart skittering.

"I've been meaning to ask, when are you and me going on a proper date, Alice?"

I titter nervously. "Oh, I don't know. We're both busy people." *Maybe when Darling Harbour freezes over.*

"And busy people need to have fun. Look, I've done the roster for the next few days. I put you down to work during the day on New Year's Eve, but I've given you the evening off." He grins exposing yellowed teeth. "We could splice the mainsail together."

Excuse me? I gag. Or at least mentally, I gag. I have no interest in splicing anything with Roger. But how to talk my way out of here? "Well, thank you. That sounds like an interesting idea, but I—"

"Great. I'll hold you to that. I'm working on pulling in a few favors, pulling a few strings ..." He taps his bulbous red nose as if he has a great secret. "If all works out, maybe that won't be all I'm pulling. We'll bung some fire in the hole yet, eh?"

I don't know about fire, but I'd like to put a rocket under him and blast him into the stratosphere. The man is a monster. I glower at him. "We can discuss this some other time. I'm too tired to think straight right now...I'm. Going. Home," I say annunciating my last words very deliberately.

There is a rumble beneath our feet — perhaps an articulated truck passing by or a small earthquake — enough to rattle the plates and dishes on the shelves and for Roger to be momentarily distracted.

Taking full advantage, I dash beneath his arm quicker than a rat can flick its tail. As I rush through the gap, a hand connects with my backside and a low jeer of laughter follows me out of the restaurant onto the dark street.

Creep!

I break into a run and don't stop until I've rounded the corner of Dalgety Road. I gasp for breath. *I can't believe the disgusting rat slapped my backside!* I'm furious and ashamed. I should report him to someone ... but who? And what would that achieve? I'd be out of a job, and even if I've no intention of staying any longer than I have to there are still bills to pay. What I need to do is persuade Twister it's time we were moving on. Sooner rather than later. Find work elsewhere. I can't stay at the Jolly Roger – scrubbing dishes is the least of my worries.

Glancing over my shoulder, as I continue to jog up the street, I can't help worrying that he could be following me. Imagine if Roger knew where we lived. Where *I* lived. A shudder runs through me. Ugh. God forbid.

Tilly has more or less moved in with her clubbing boyfriend. I don't really blame her. It must be much nicer sharing silk sheets and a king-sized waterbed with Axel, than sharing the lumpy futon and cramped studio flat with me. Still, I can't help wishing she was around a bit more.

If wishes were horses, beggars would ride. Mum's voice in my head makes me smile and I finally slow down to a walk.

The last time I saw Twister was Christmas morning. I made the mistake of bringing up the subject of our truncated gap year and travel plans, and a row exploded between us in spectacular festive fashion. It's nothing unusual for the two of us to bicker, but that had been about as close as we've come yet to going our separate ways – something I promised Mum would never happen. For all the stress and headaches my sister gives me, I adore her. It's about time I called a truce. Or at least attempt to make contact with her.

I take out my cellphone and call her, but she doesn't answer. Maybe she's still pissed off with me. Maybe she's too busy having a life. Maybe it shouldn't always be me having to—

All holy crap! I leap out of my skin as something darts across my path and hisses — a bloody cat.

My heart pummels against my ribcage and I bend double trying to catch my breath. "Bloody scaredy cat!" I yell after it.

A sob escapes me.

It takes a few deep breaths and a stern talking to myself and blowing my nose, before I get my nerves back under control. If anyone was watching me they'd think I'd lost the plot entirely.

I start walking again and my legs feel like jelly. I wanted this adventure, I remind myself. I wanted nothing more than to see the world and live ... but some days I feel like I might as well be on my own. I never realized traveling with Twister would mean spending so much time alone...

♡♡♡

Want to find out what happens to Alice? Read here:
Alice in Wanderlust.

NEW BOOK ON ITS WAY...

For fans of close proximity, fake dates and holiday romances...

After 'Alice in Wanderlust', escape with this roadtrip romcom 'Alice and the Impossible Game'.

Get here

Printed in Great Britain
by Amazon